N

for Every

Eye

Not for Every Eye

A NOVEL *by* GÉRARD BESSETTE

Translated from the French
by GLEN SHORTLIFFE

TORONTO
Exile Editions

1994

Originally Published in French as LE LIBRAIRE
by René Julliard, Paris, 1960

Text Copyright © GÉRARD BESSETTE 1984, 1999
Translation © GLEN SHORTLIFFE 1994, 1999
Copyright © EXILE EDITIONS LIMITED 1994, 1999

This edition is published by Exile Editions Limited,
20 Dale Avenue, Toronto, Ontario, Canada   M4W 1K4

SALES DISTRIBUTION:
McArthur & Company
c/o Harper Collins
1995 Markham Road
Toronto, ON
M1B 5M8
toll free:
1 800 387 0117
1 800 668 5788 (fax)

Composed at MOONS OF JUPITER, Toronto
Printed and Bound by MARC VEILLEUX IMPRIMEUR, Quebec

The publisher wishes to acknowledge
the assistance toward publication of the Canada Council
and the Ontario Arts Council.

The Canada Council
Conseil des Arts du Canada

ISBN 1-55096-549-2

March 10

My first move on arriving in Saint Joachim was to find myself a room. With only about fifty dollars left in my pocket I wanted to avoid spending the night at a hotel. I know myself too well: once ensconced in a hotel room I should have stayed on indefinitely.

I got out of the bus dead tired. In the little restaurant that does service as a bus terminal I bought myself some cigars. As the girl handed me my change I noticed lying on a shelf a copy of the local weekly *Le Courrier de Saint Joachim*, and I picked it up. It was three days old, but this was of no consequence.

Making my way to a wooden bench in a corner, I opened the paper to the classified ads. There were just under a dozen rooms listed for rent, and when I had jotted these addresses down in my notebook I asked the waitress for a plan of the city. Apparently surprised by such a request, she scratched her forehead in momentary puzzlement before turning to ruffle through a drawer filled with odd sheets of paper, from which she eventually extracted a yellowed map. She thought it necessary to warn me that it was several years old, and pointed out that I could get a more recent one at Léon's Book Shop. But I was to present myself next day at this very establishment to take up my duties as a clerk, and I had no desire to put in an appearance ahead of time. I assured her that the old map would do me quite nicely.

I installed myself in a booth and spread the map out on the formica-topped table. The topography of Saint Joachim was not complicated. The avenues, almost all bearing the names of saints, stood in even rows running north and south parallel to the little green river, which interrupted its wanderings at this point as though on purpose. The streets cut the avenues at right angles and were numbered from First to Twenty-eighth on the map. I say "on the map" because I have since noticed that their number has almost doubled since the publication of that document in 1936. For me this had no importance anyway. I knew that Léon's Book Shop was centrally located on Fourteenth Street; I hate moving about and I wanted a lodging as close as possible to my work.

Of the eleven rooms advertised two were for women only and six for men, the remainder being open to either. Of those theoretically available to me I was able to isolate six on the map. It occurred to me briefly to establish an itinerary for each of the two relevant categories: men only on the one hand, men or women on the other. But this procedure would have almost doubled the distance to be covered. I gave up the idea.

Having settled upon my route, I checked my suitcase with the waitress, at the same time making a gesture toward paying for the use of the map. She told me to keep it; she had no use for it. Aside from commercial travellers and relatives of the inhabitants, few strangers stopped off in Saint Joachim. I was the exception – but no doubt I came on business? Ordinarily I never answer questions of this sort, but this girl had shown me some kindness, so I allowed that in a sense one might say I came on business provided the word were broadly interpreted. This reply seemed to go beyond her and she tossed her head in renewed perplexity.

At the first two houses I was told that the rooms were already rented. This was probably the truth. I say "probably" because it is not out of the question that I was turned down on account of my appearance, particularly my clothes. My felt hat, dutifully raised the instant each door was opened, bore several improbable contusions and a greasy streak which could hardly escape an attentive eye. The sleeves of my topcoat were frayed at the edges and my scarf was not as clean as it might be. Though not the ugliest man in the world, I have a pale, sagging face with deep wrinkles cutting the length of my cheeks. Nonetheless I am presentable enough and I can state my case with a certain persuasiveness, as evidenced by the fact that I proved acceptable at the next two addresses. This time I was the one to beg off, not so much because of the rooms as because of the attending matrons, who tried to pump me for personal information.

I have had no reason to regret this decision. The room I now occupy satisfies me fully. It is not large, but what does that matter? As a matter of fact it is exactly eleven by eight and a half feet; I measured it one evening when I had nothing to do. By this I mean one evening before I adopted my present routine. In point of fact I never have anything to do in the evening.

My problem is to kill time. Inasmuch as I am too tired to go walking after work this is not easy. When you can walk all you like you can always manage, even in a small place like Saint

Joachim. You stroll along the main streets; you stare into the shop windows or gaze at other strollers. You go over to the station or the terminal at train and bus times; you sit around and listen to the gossip. But when you lack the energy for long walks and you know you can't get to sleep before the early hours of the morning, then killing time becomes a major difficulty.

That is why, at the end of my short evening constitutional, I always settle wearily into a corner of the beer parlour. Not an ideal solution, I know; but I cannot bear the notion of entombing myself in one or another of Saint Joachim's three movie houses, all of them filthy holes, two with nothing better than wooden seats and the third insufficiently heated. On the other hand I also dislike staying alone in my room. I gave up reading quite some time ago. For music I should have to buy a radio and I am not sure I should like it. No, in my case the beer parlour is definitely the best solution.

Aside from the hotel beverage room, which is situated next to a noisy dance hall that gives me a headache, there are three other drinking places in Saint Joachim. They are all about the same. If, after feeling them all out, I finally fixed on Trefflé's, it is because this establishment is located only ten minutes away from Léon's Book Shop and from my room, in an out-of-the-way district where I am unlikely to run into my customers. The place is frequented mainly by workmen, and these can be quite rowdy on occasion, especially Friday and Saturday nights. But they leave me to myself.

I usually stow myself in a corner, up against a hot-air duct and right next to the toilets. With each swing of the door, of course, the opening exhales a rather dubious aroma, but this is the warmest place and the one that requires the least physical exertion when I have to go and relieve myself. Besides, I am beginning to get used to the smell; I smoke a few more cigars, that is all. On the whole I am reasonably content with my sessions in the beer parlour.

The only serious annoyance is that my constitution takes rather poorly to beer. Let me be clear: it is not the intake that bothers me; it is the elimination. After the seventh or eighth glass I begin to experience a burning sensation in the bladder. For some days I really thought I should have to give up beer altogether, but while leafing through the paper I came across an advertisement for a really remarkable antacid salt called "Safe-All", and I bought a bottle. A good dose of this preparation somewhere between the third and fifth glass reduces my discomfort to a mild tingling.

At first thought it might seem simpler not to drink at all, or at any rate to drink less, for in no sense am I an alcoholic. Before coming here I drank very little on the whole, except at class reunions, and fortunately these occur only once a year. But no matter: I did not begin this diary for the purpose of raking over old memories. I took it up to fill in the time on Sundays, when the beer parlours are closed. . . . I was explaining the why and wherefore of my libations. To be fair, I must recognize that Trefflé's waiters have nothing to do with it. They don't press you to order. They come and get my glass when it's empty, but they never ask me whether I want another. I do not say that they act this way through altruism, but the fact remains that it is my own finger which is raised, of my own free will, whenever my glass is empty. Then the waiter comes and places two more glasses before me. I give him twenty-five cents – twenty for the beer and five for the tip – and he thanks me and goes away. This unobtrusiveness on the part of the help was one of my reasons for choosing *Chez Trefflé* rather than *Le Baril* or *Le Bon Buveur*.

To all appearances, then, I am under no external pressure. Still, the circumstances must be borne in mind. For one thing I take up a whole table to myself, having warned the waiters that I do not care for company. Then too it must not be forgotten that I spend an average of seven hours a day in Trefflé's. Under the circumstances I cannot help feeling a certain moral obligation to consume a fair amount.

At all events I have now reached an average of twenty glasses per evening, without ill effects other than the one previously mentioned. Of course I didn't rise to these heights in a single evening. Starting from six or eight glasses it took me three weeks to climb progressively up to my present level.

But enough of that. None of these musings affects the matter at hand in the slightest. Let us get down to the circumstances that have brought me to Saint Joachim. On second thought, no, not today. It is getting late and my arm is tired.

March 17

To begin, then, at the beginning. Early in February, having been unemployed for almost two months and being down to my last fifty dollars, I decided to look for work. I went down to the government employment office and took a look at the bulletin board. Several lumberjacks were wanted, an assortment of commercial travellers, two mechanics, three lathe operators, half a dozen book-keepers, some dishwashers and a few labourers. In short, nothing very tempting. I asked one of the unemployed standing near by whether that was all there was. He said no: additional lists were kept in the offices, there being insufficient space to post all of them. Then he asked me whether I had my card. This was the first time I had heard of such a thing. The card in question is a small certificate given out by the employment office attesting that the applicant has no criminal record and is looking for work "in good faith". This expression struck me as absurd; I couldn't conceive how it was possible to look for work "in bad faith". But this was mere inexperience on my part. The fellow explained to me that many of the jobless report to the office for the sole purpose of getting their unemployment insurance, and that they continually manage to evade any work offered. This impressed me as an ingenious arrangement, and I was sorry not to be able to resort to it myself. Unfortunately in my capacity as a tutor at Saint Etienne School, "a charitable institution", I was not protected by unemployment insurance.

It appeared at all events that to get a card I had to submit to an interview. The prospect aroused no enthusiasm in me, but as I was rather tired I sat down on the bench next to the other fellow, and I waited. There were at least fifteen people ahead of us. As these were called in one by one the rest of us slid the seats of our pants along the bench, adding our bit to the well-worn polish of the wood. My companion had lapsed into silence. He seemed nervous. He was afraid of not getting his card stamped. I remember lighting a cigar and drawing a few puffs; then I fell asleep.

A few minutes later a dig from my neighbour's elbow jolted me awake and I opened my eyes. At first I thought it must be my turn to be interviewed, and it struck me that I hadn't had long to wait. But I was mistaken. I looked up to see a fat character in a navy-blue suit standing over me with his hand extended.

"How're things, Hervé?" he asked me. "Haven't seen you for ages. What's become of you anyway? Still in the teaching profession?"

I recognized Martin Nault, a former classmate. Just my luck. Nault, a long pointed chin attached to the mug of an ex-pug, had always struck me as peculiarly repulsive. I pretended not to see his outstretched hand and answered indifferently that I had given up teaching.

"Oh, yes," said Nault, scratching his chin, "I remember now. Who was it told me? ... Oh, yes, it was Massé. He went over to the school to see you, and you'd left. ..."

It didn't surprise me that Nault knew all about it. He's the kind of idiot who goes for class gossip and memories of "the old Alma Mater" the way certain country-folk thirst for news of cousins eight times removed that they've never even met. Another one of the unemployed had just been called in and I slid another space along the bench, ignoring Nault altogether. But he wasn't thrown off that easily. I must explain that my classmates have always taken me for a cynical odd-ball; so much so that I can show them the worst discourtesies without their taking offence. There was a time when I enjoyed cultivating this role, for it is always pleasant to be able to insult others with impunity. But it also entails some disadvantages – as now, for instance, when the problem was to get rid of a goddamn bore. Never had I realized this more acutely than at this moment when Nault stood over me, belly and buttocks heaving, face beaming, while he surveyed me with a condescension that was not unmixed with anticipation at the prospect of hearing all about my failures and frustrations.

"What are you doing here?" he asked, perceiving that I showed no inclination to engage in conversation.

I took plenty of time to relight my cigar before replying that I was there because I liked the surroundings, that their luxuriousness appealed to me.

The fact is that this employment office occupied pretty slummy quarters. Dirty grey walls, sooty window-panes, floors covered with a chipped linoleum, the total effect was reminiscent of the waiting-room of a back-country railway station.

Nault exploded in a deep rich laugh. My reply hadn't nettled him in the slightest. He put his hand on my shoulder, a fat paw overgrown with a black fleece.

"Come on into my office," he said. "We can chat in peace in there."

I rose to my feet and followed him, I'm not too sure why. I suspect it was because since the appearance of Nault my neighbour had been jostling me with his elbow and clearing his throat to attract attention. Obviously he wanted an introduction. As I learned a few minutes later, Nault was Assistant Director of the office. But for all of me the fellow could damn well look out for himself. Rather than get involved in that I even preferred an interview with Nault.

Hardly had we sat down in his office – which, I noted with satisfaction, was only slightly less shoddy than the waiting-room – when Nault resumed his interrogation.

"Well then, so you've left the good fathers of Saint Etienne? What are you doing now?"

He rubbed his great hairy hands together and a greedy smile appeared on his lips. He was already licking his chops over the prospect of reporting my misfortunes to our former class-mates. So I told him that at the moment I was president of a university, but that I was thinking seriously of changing my position, inasmuch as my secretaries, a pair of costive old maids, refused to let me fiddle around with the co-eds as conscientiously as I'd have liked. Nault doubled up with laughter at this idiotic reply. This is the kind of "wit" that has earned me my reputation among my classmates.

"And what sort of position do you have in mind?" Nault asked, when his attack of hilarity had subsided.

I answered that it was all the same to me provided I didn't have to do anything.

After a renewed outburst of guffaws Nault began to rub his chin reflectively. It was clear that he wanted to help me, but without compromising his own prestige. I didn't blame him for nursing some doubts as to my suitability as an applicant. Neither my clothes nor my deportment were such as to inspire confidence in an employer. For some time past I had had no opportunity to renew my wardrobe, as the saying goes. As an "educationist" I had almost been expected to appear eternally clad in the same shabby attire, and people had given up commenting on it. They contented themselves with paying me a starvation wage and letting me stagnate in the junior classes.

Suddenly Nault's grotesque countenance lit up, and he snapped his stubby fingers in a gesture of triumph.

"You like books as much as ever?"

Half-pursing my lips in indifference I told him that though books wouldn't burn as long as coal, still I sometimes used them when no other fuel was at hand.

Nault unleashed his laugh again, then abruptly wreathed his features in the serious mask of an Assistant Director.

"Look," he said, "I know a guy, a bookseller, who's looking for somebody....How would that strike you?..." He turned to a little card-index. "The only disadvantage is that it's a bit far from Montreal, in Saint Joachim...."

No point in prolonging the account of this comic-opera interview. I accepted the offer. Saint Joachim or elsewhere, it was all one to me. Nault telephoned immediately to Léon Chicoine to let him know that he was sending him "someone real good who's a whiz when it comes to books". I didn't know then that Léon Chicoine was an old friend of Nault's, nor that at one time, during the depression, Nault had lent him a few thousand dollars to refloat his business. If I had known, perhaps I wouldn't have taken the job. Perhaps, I say, for who knows? Anyway it makes little difference now. Here I am, and I expect I'll stay as long as things work out. I hardly feel in the mood to move again. And besides, I'm anxious to see how my little adventure is going to turn out, the one involving the books that are "not for everyone's eyes", as Léon Chicoine puts it. . . .

But let us proceed in order: first of all the setting. . . . But I'll get to that next week.

March 24

Léon's Book Store – books, stationery, religious articles, toys – consists of a long, narrow room lined with shelving, and a dusty back room that serves the proprietor as an office. To the left of this office is a padlocked door which I had at first supposed must lead to some unusable part of the building. Instead, it opens into a sort of out-size closet, which M. Léon, drawing to the full upon his capacity for sententious unoriginality, has christened his *sanctum sanctorum*. But more about this later.

The shop as such is divided into four departments. To the left of the entrance, religious articles: rosaries, medals, works of piety, and the like. Left rear, toys and greeting cards. Front right, stationery, pencils, fountain pens, notebooks, etc.

Finally, just opposite the toys, my own department of "secular" books.

Actually, these so-called departments are indistinguishable save by the merchandise they display. The shelving is unbroken by any partition, the approximate boundaries between sections being indicated only by four narrow counters of polished oak which stretch out from each side of the shop. The book department, "over the destinies of which I preside", to use the phrase of M. Léon Chicoine, is the most comfortable of the four. Located some distance from the entrance, it offers the double advantage of being the least subject to draughts and the least attractive to customers.

Religious articles are watched over by Mlle Galarneau, a dried-up old maid with an egg-bound pucker of perpetual disapproval. Her department shows the biggest turnover, but Mlle Placide (toys) maintains that hers makes more money, inasmuch as objects of piety go mainly to religious communities enjoying substantial discounts, and thus show a slender margin of profit. I haven't picked up many details on the stationery department. Mlle Morin runs this one, an arid, bony little person, remarkably taciturn by nature. So much the better, for her tight-lipped bearing helps to hold in check the chatter of the other two. Not that it muzzles them completely, unfortunately; but by a singular stroke of luck Mlles Galarneau (religion) and Placide (toys) have been "not speaking" for God knows how long, so they never say a word to each other save "on official business" or in the immediate presence of our lord and master Léon Chicoine.

As I can be every bit as uncommunicative as Mlle Morin, I manage to get through my daily eight hours among these three old maids in relative peace and quiet – relative, I say, for I am still compelled to emit the odd grunt from time to time in response to queries from Mlles Galarneau (piety) and Placide (playthings).

Mlle Galarneau, for her part, takes a rather dim view of me, as the saying goes. It seems she has a brother, a rural postman with a passion for pocket novels, and he had been after my job. Mlle Placide (toys) hastened to let me in on this on the very morning of my arrival. In fact it led her initially to view me as a natural ally in her battle against her arch-enemy Mlle Galarneau. Her enthusiasm has cooled since. One day she asked me to help her to set out some toys, but I told her flatly that that wasn't my baby, which hurt her feelings. So what? Let her see to her own problems. No pouting of hers is going to keep me awake nights. . . .

All in all, I'd be fairly well satisfied with my daily surroundings if it weren't for the customers. God, those customers! The Joachimites are big husky fellows with powerful lungs. They talk as though everyone else were deaf. The ones from the country are the worst of the lot – we get some in from the country now and then looking for statues and rosaries. Is it their habit of bellowing at animals, or just plain stupidity? I have no idea, and have given the matter no thought. It's enough to have to listen to them. My own customers in the book department are generally a little more civilized, Joachimites though they be, and somewhat less thunderous in their vocal effects. Because of this I usually manage somehow to while away a good part of the day in quiet dozing.

Léon Chicoine himself strikes me so far as being a good enough fellow. Tight-fisted if you like (I make forty dollars a week), pretentious too, not to say sententious, grandiloquent, and rather hypocritical; but a good fellow just the same, and not as stupid as one might be tempted to believe at first sight. Above all, he possesses the great quality of being absent most of the time. Ordinarily he arrives at the book store about a quarter to five to count the daily receipts and deposit them in the little safe in his office. It must be said that he has been very clever in organizing his business. When it comes to conscientiousness, honesty, interest in the firm, and affability toward the customer, his staff is irreproachable. Except myself, of course; and in my own case I have now come to realize that M. Chicoine didn't hire me just out of friendship for Nault. He had an idea in the back of his head. I'll come back to that too.

Anyway, the rivalry among the three maiden ladies is remarkably keen. They vie with each other constantly to keep the best department, the most attractive display, the largest number of customers. I have no idea by what device M. Chicoine keeps them on their toes. Certainly he is not the type to be lavish with either praise or blame. Yet it takes only an approving nod or a mere frown to set the three old maids – even the taciturn Mlle Morin (stationery) – flushing with delight or mortification. For me this is a blasted nuisance. It would be going too far to say that it makes me keep my department orderly, but I do feel obliged to set some limits on the confusion. On this point M. Chicoine has been quite decent so far. He said to me once while replacing a book:

"I don't think books ought to be so carefully set out as religious objects. Otherwise it tends to scare off the customers, don't you think? They would hesitate to browse around for fear of upsetting the arrangement.... Of course, the opposite extreme must also be avoided. Customers have to be able to find what they're after. What do you think, M. Jodoin?"

I was tempted to reply that the kind of customers we had to deal with were hardly worth knocking yourself out for, but I thought it wiser to nod my head without comment.

Apart from his daily rifling of the tills, M. Chicoine's sole function in the business consists in ordering new stock. In the case of items we already handle, each of us is expected to hand in a complete weekly report listing those out of stock or in short supply. Another damn nuisance, of course, but I suppose there's no way round it if you want to stay in business.

Well then, so far as Léon Chicoine is concerned, I have little cause for complaint. The shoppers are something else again. In the first place they have a way of being plural, while the boss is singular. In all fairness I suppose this is not the fault of the individual customer, though it does represent a major obstacle. Given half a chance, I am willing enough to overlook it, as evidenced by the fact that some of them do manage to avoid getting on my nerves. When they know what they want and ask for it right away I give it to them, take their money, put it in the cash drawer, then go back and sit down. Either that or I tell them we haven't got it. So far, so good. Even the browsers don't bother me particularly, as they wander up and down the lengths of the shelves opening and closing books, provided they go about it quietly. I simply ignore them, which is easy to do thanks to a big opaque visor that I pull down over my eyes. I figure they'll eventually make up their minds what they want or else clear out without bothering me.

But the ones I find it hard to put up with are the unshakable leeches who insist on regarding me as a literary consultant and purveyor of general information. The only thing that keeps me from throwing them out is the thought that I'd have to move again if I got too rough with them. "What do you think of such-and-such a writer? Have you read such-and-such a book? Is this a romantic love story? Which of these two is the more interesting, do you think?" Despite the physical effort that would be involved in such an operation, I am constantly tempted to apply my boot to the rear of these sickening inquisitors. But I can't risk it. I must be content to choose for them the books best calculated to bore them to death. Of course this requires some mental exertion on my part, which is a bit of a strain; but then you never get anything for nothing. Obviously I can't suggest the right titles without first getting some notion of how their tastes run, so I can't avoid the bother of asking them a few questions. I console myself with the thought that my efforts in this direction are a contribution to future peace and quiet, and I will say I've had very few repeaters. True enough, there are some who return to the attack a few days later with the declaration that they found the book dull. In these cases I quiz them on the precise portions that struck them as particularly scandalous or soporific, and I hand them another volume as similar as possible to the first. The joke is that this procedure has enabled me to palm off on my public a whole flock of dusty turkeys that had been roosting on the shelves for years, an accomplishment which earned me a word of congratulation from M. Chicoine. That is what is called killing two birds with one stone.

However, the trick didn't come off in the case of one of my customers, a certain Mlle Anasthasie Lessort, a maiden lady with a helpless old father to look after. She had asked me to pick out "a cheerful novel – you know, something with a little optimism in it". I immediately recommended Carco's *Jésus-la-Caille*. The title seemed to inspire confidence and she accepted the book without protest, imagining it perhaps to be some kind of Life of Christ. Well, three days later she was back, and overflowing with gratitude! Before reading the book she had found her life "useless, insipid, full of worry and frustration, you know". Now she felt almost happy. She thanked God she'd been born in Saint Joachim instead of in Paris, and she invoked the mercy of Heaven upon such unfortunates as Jésus-la-Caille. Certain passages, it was true, had escaped her – "what with the slang and all that, you know". Perhaps I could help her out a bit on that score? All this gave me a stiff jolt, as the saying goes, and I hastened to assure her that slang was not my strong point. Nevertheless, she begged me to recommend another volume. My first impulse was to refuse, but, thinking better of it, I laid hold of the thickest tome that came to hand, and assured her that she would find it first class. I haven't seen her for the past two weeks, so she must have got bogged down in it somewhere. Either that or her dear old father is finally on his death-bed. All to the good, either way.

But why go on? It's bad enough to have to put up with such customers as mine six days a week without mulling over their peculiarities on my day off. I must really be hard up for something to write about when I bother describing such trivialities. But what else is there? It is that or nothing. Having no imagination at all, I am incapable of making things up. My past life is something I'd just as soon forget, so, with only the present to deal with, it all comes down to the same thing whether I talk about my customers or something else. As long as they are not around, that's the main thing.

Besides, my department doesn't exactly overflow with them. In fact, I believe I have noticed a certain falling off since I took over. Let's hope the trend continues. The trouble is that Léon Chicoine's is the only book store to speak of in Saint Joachim. Here as elsewhere, of course, the drug stores and restaurants display their racks of pocket books, but there is nothing else.

When the shelves are full in my department and the aisles are empty, that's the way I like it. Then, ensconced on my stool behind the counter, chin in hands, visor pulled well down, I spend my time doing nothing. I simply wait for closing time at five-thirty. It's astonishing how quickly time passes when you do nothing. Provided you are not free, of course. I mean provided some "duty" or other keeps you tied to your post;

otherwise it does not work. Take myself, for instance: if I were not driven to it by the need to earn my living in Léon's Book Shop, I should be quite incapable of spending several hours on end perched on a stool.

When I say I do nothing, what I mean is that I do not move. Of course I am thinking, after a fashion. That is, images drift through my mind. That kind of thing can't be helped. It's human nature.

But enough of that. Let us come to a more important subject, the *sanctum sanctorum*. I have already mentioned, I think, that the closet to which Milord Chicoine has attached this pompous title is hidden away at the back of the shop behind a door that looks as though it led nowhere. From the outside nothing gives any indication that this "closet" is in fact a room about six feet square, which must certainly encroach upon the neighbouring building. But let us proceed in order. . . . I shall leave that for next Sunday.

March 31

Three weeks ago I didn't even know this dark room existed. I don't recall having paid any particular attention to that massive oak door with its big padlock. I'm not inquisitive by nature, and I should rate my powers of observation close to zero. But no matter. Now that I think it over, I realize that for two weeks previous to the "unveiling of the *sanctum sanctorum*" M. Chicoine was busily pursuing his "little inquiry as to my convictions". This is the very expression he used when he finally made up his mind to "talk seriously" to me.

One evening about five-thirty, just after the departure of the three old maids, Léon Chicoine apparently decided that "the time had come". He politely asked me into his office, where he began by congratulating me on the efficiency of my work – still having in mind, perhaps, the small herd of white elephants I had managed to liquidate. He went on to inquire whether I had found our collection of books fairly complete. I replied that he knew the local market better than I did and that consequently I felt I had nothing to offer on the subject.

"But haven't you noticed the absence of particular works, works of certain writers who are ... well, important?"

I confess the question caught me by surprise. Léon Chicoine is not the sort to keep you in his office discussing literature. However, I ventured the remark that, if I was not mistaken, the Montreal book stores where I once was wont to browse did indeed possess a fuller stock than his. M. Chicoine appeared to find this reply very much to his liking. He nodded approvingly and drew a bunch of keys from his pocket. Opening a drawer, he deposited on the desk a bottle of Scotch and two glasses.

"You'll join me in a bit of something before you leave?"

I allowed that I didn't mind if I did.

"I know you prefer beer," he went on as he poured out the drinks, "but it's impossible to keep any here. You can't keep it cool, and nothing tastes worse than warm beer, don't you agree?"

I corroborated his opinion with the assertion that cold beer did indeed taste better than warm beer. M. Chicoine approved with another nod and tossed off his glass in a single gulp. I followed his example. He poured out two more and resumed:

"As you say, my collection is no doubt not as complete as in some Montreal book stores, but it's not as insignificant as you might imagine, either ..."

I interrupted to point out that I hadn't said his collection was insignificant, that everything was relative anyway, and that any view I might have of the matter, not having conducted a detailed examination of his stock, was necessarily based solely upon the experience of three weeks' employment, during which I had rarely been asked for any volume we didn't have on our shelves.

"But in those few cases did you notice the *kind* of book that was asked for?" he persisted.

I confessed I had not, but I added that it would take me only a moment to get the list of these books, which I had kept in my cash drawer.

With one hand he gestured to me not to bother, while with the other he filled our glasses for the third time. A rosy glow was beginning to suffuse his waxy skin, and his eyes held an unaccustomed gleam.

"Monsieur Jodoin," he went on solemnly, "even without consulting that list I'd lay you two to one that in most cases the books concerned are the kind that aren't for everybody's eyes."

I answered that this was quite possible. I thought of *Jésus-la-Caille*, which I had given to Mlle Lessort, and remembering that we still had a few copies in stock, I mentioned the incident to M. Chicoine, mainly to prove that I was still following the conversation.

"Carco," he retorted, "is not on the Index. There is no mention of him either in Sagehomme or in Bethléem. It's true that my own editions of these references may be a bit out of date..."

He broke off and fixed my eyes with his own. No doubt he was expecting some kind of revealing reaction, but I failed to see how this item of information concerned me, so I contented myself with taking another gulp of Scotch. It was the real stuff.

"Has any reader been complaining about *Jésus-la-Caille*?"

I shook my head.

"Then there's no need for you to bother your head about it."

I broke in to assure him that this was the least of my worries, but he was intent on pursuing the point:

"As long as the customers don't say anything, I don't see that it's up to me to supervise their reading. Books are a commercial product like any other."

I went along with that, which seemed to satisfy him. He emptied his glass and got to his feet. Making his way to the

23

wash-stand in the corner he ran the tap for a few moments and returned with a decanter of water. When he had downed a large gulp, he launched into a tortuous explanation of the nature of the book trade, which, he maintained, was "somewhat special and delicate, you might say", compared with any other business. Social circumstances had to be considered, for example, as well as the prevailing psychological climate. As these "intangibles" exercised a direct influence on the law of supply and demand, it behooved us (did it not?) to study them from this angle. Morality itself, indeed, was entitled to its place in such considerations. (Did I not agree? Quite so.) But on the other hand – and here M. Chicoine erected a skinny forefinger – for men of principle like ourselves, for minds "passionately devoted to freedom of thought", it was no less imperative (right?) to grant the greatest possible latitude to individual choice. What did I think?

To tell the truth I didn't think anything at all, and in fact had been giving only half an ear to his oration. Years ago, during my student days, I had of course sounded off like everyone else on the relation of morality to literature. Youth will be served. But today such discussions put me to sleep.

It seemed somehow out of character for M. Chicoine to want to draw me into an exploration of this sort of sophistry. He had always struck me as a realist little given to speculations of the kind. Besides, as I have remarked, I had been only half listening, so I wasn't too clear on what he was getting at. At the same time I had the definite impression that in one way or another he was appealing to me for help.

"What do you think?" he persisted, this time a little breathlessly.

I could have drawn him out on the precise nature of his position. He would have worked himself into a corner for sure. But what was the use? I answered that he was absolutely right.

Léon Chicoine rubbed his long bony hands together.

"I'm delighted to hear you say so!" he exclaimed. "I was sure you were the sort of man who knows life, a man who believes in individual freedom. You *do* believe in it, don't you?"

Of course his question was so vague as to be meaningless, but I duly declared that I did indeed believe in individual freedom, and this answer seemed to supply the last bit of reassurance he needed. With great deliberation he set his glass back on the desk, selected another key from his jangling collection, and directed his steps toward the *sanctum sanctorum*. When he had opened the door he turned to find me still sitting at the desk enjoying my Scotch. His voice as he called me over to have a look betrayed some impatience. He had been expecting more curiosity on my part, and I suppose I ought to have jollied him along by following at his elbow. But who cares? Glass in hand, I walked into the *sanctum sanctorum*.

As I have already indicated, this room must certainly impinge upon the area of the neighbouring shop. Perhaps some former occupant of both buildings had had this communicating door cut in the partition. From the inside the room has the appearance of a basement, with its cement-block walls, unbroken by window or grating, and its vague odour of mildew. All in all, a cheerless place, uncompromisingly stern in aspect despite the shelves of books and the big milky globe of the central light fixture.

Fortunately, the first time I set foot in it I was fortified by a good snootful of Scotch. I hastened to toss down another shot to put a little starch into my backbone.

M. Chicoine, his arms spread out in the attitude of a new

millionaire showing off his estates, was clearly in ecstasy.

"Well, now! What do you think of this, Monsieur Jodoin?" he asked triumphantly. "I'll bet you're a bit surprised, heh? I don't suppose you expected to find such a collection as this in a small town like Saint Joachim?"

I gathered that he expected me to take a look along the shelves at this point, so I obediently did so. In a rapid glance I caught the names of a few writers, like Gide, Maeterlinck, Renan, Voltaire, Zola...

"Eh? What do you say to that now?" he demanded again. His eyes glittered as he sought to gauge my reaction.

His whole attitude struck me as childishly silly. It would have been so simple to place these books in the shop with all the others. After all, this wasn't the Collège Saint Etienne, and Chicoine was surely master in his own house.

"Well, what do you say?"

I replied that he had more books than I had thought, and that his collection seemed to me to be quite complete.

Léon Chicoine scrutinized me with an air of surprise, even concern, perhaps more because of my tone of utter boredom than because of the words themselves. But, thinking no doubt that he had now gone too far to draw back, he felt impelled to emphasize his position more aggressively:

"Maybe you think I keep this stock just to make money? Well, you're wrong! Quite the contrary. I keep it because I believe in individual freedom."

When this elicited nothing but another shrug, his tone became still more combative:

"In case you should take it into your head to spread this around, let me warn you right now that I'll flatly deny absolutely everything. We'll see which one of us will be believed, a new arrival like you, or a man like me with a first-class reputation among the townspeople – and I need

26

scarcely add that such a breach of confidence would mark the end of your employment here."

This time it was my turn to scrutinize him. The look of him amazed me. His face had lost its colour and waves of nervous twitching agitated his flabby cheeks. His eyes, so piercing as he stared at me a moment before, now wavered wildly between me and the shelves of books. I realized abruptly that he was afraid. What other reason could he possibly have to attack me like this, to take me for a spy, to threaten me with dismissal?

At that moment, instead of getting angry and returning a sharp answer, I suddenly felt for Léon Chicoine a kind of sympathy that was close to compassion. Without stopping to think I blurted out:

"Monsieur Chicoine, I've been working for you for three weeks and you've never tried to restrict my freedom. Every night of the week, as I'm sure you know, I go to the beer parlour and drink till closing time. Others might have complained. Not once have you made any remarks about it at all. This is the kind of liberty I appreciate at its full value. Now you show me a collection of books that are officially taboo around here. You want me to sell them? All right, I'll sell them – and you can rely on my discretion."

I stopped, surprised at my own verbosity. The flat nasal voice that had been a constant target for the ragging of my students must in that moment have taken on an accent of sincerity, perhaps even a kind of eloquence. At all events without a word M. Chicoine clasped me by the hand.

We must have made a ridiculous spectacle, standing there motionless for a full thirty seconds, hand in hand in the middle of the *sanctum sanctorum*.

M. Chicoine was the first to recover his senses. He released my hand and held out the key to the room. Then he set about explaining to me that these books were to be sold only to "serious purchasers", and then only after the greatest circumspection.

After the drama of the handshake – laughable if you like, but perhaps not entirely devoid of a certain nobility – it struck me that the boss was getting down to practical details a little quickly. I felt some annoyance, partly, no doubt, because I was embarrassed by my own outburst, a bit ashamed to have let myself go like that. I asked him rather roughly exactly what he meant by "serious purchasers". He looked nonplussed for a moment, then launched into a confused explanation from which it emerged essentially that a "serious purchaser" was one to whom it would be safe to sell such books.

Of course he didn't say this in so many words. He talked of freedom of thought and the right to knowledge, he referred to the immaturity of our population, the stuffiness of our censors, and so on. I hardly listened. Not that I disagreed, but it struck me he spoke without any real conviction.

By way of peroration he went into the reasons which compelled him to price these books some seventy-five to a hundred per cent above the others: the slow turnover which kept a considerable part of his capital tied up, "not to mention the other risks. . . ."

These questions didn't interest me in the slightest, and I said so. I asked only that the *sanctum sanctorum* should not be a purely commercial enterprise. Otherwise, after all, what was the use of it? Besides, I was beginning to feel utterly worn out. I put the key in my pocket and left.

The fresh air did me good, restoring me to such spirits that for the first time in months, if not years, I found myself caressing the innocent notion that perhaps after all I was not yet completely useless, that perhaps my life might still have a meaning. This was not reasoned out, of course. But much as I tried to tell myself that it was only the Scotch, an afterglow of my exaltation of a few moments before, a mere fantasy to be firmly nipped in the bud, still the feeling clung to me.

So much so that when I entered Trefflé's that night, an hour and a half late, I nodded my head toward my neighbour, known to all as Old Man Manseau. Like myself he is one of the regulars, so I had seen him every day for a month, but without ever speaking to him. He turned his tanned, rough-hewn countenance upon me and grunted a response. Then his knotted, rheumatic hands closed upon his glass and his rasping voice pronounced a toast:

"To your good health, Monsieur Jodoin."

"Thank you, Monsieur Manseau. Same to you."

That was the sum total of our conversation. Old Man Manseau is not given to idle chatter and neither am I. We simply wanted to establish good neighbourly relations. That done, having nothing more to say, we said nothing.

Since then, every time I see Old Man Manseau – which means every day of the week except Sunday – I nod my head in his direction. He grunts a reply and raises his glass a few inches off the table. When the time comes to leave he utters another monosyllable as he gets to his feet, and I tell him good-night.

April 7

Except when absolutely necessary I haven't struck up a conversation with anyone since leaving Saint Etienne School. One exception is my landlady, Mme Bouthiller. With her it does sometimes happen that I am the first to speak. Not often, but it does happen. I don't put much into it though, for she irritates me a little. . . .

Boredom accounts for many things. Mme Bouthiller is the clinging type, true enough, but in moderation. When you come right down to it, I'm really not too sure what she wants of me. Not that I have given the matter any thought, of course. No doubt it is mere curiosity on her part. As for myself, I'm polite to her, nothing more, which seems to fan her desire to know more about me – so as to be able to gabble about it with the neighbours, I expect. Strangers are rare birds in Saint

Joachim and by taking one in she has acquired a certain prestige. At the same time she is expected to keep the neighbourhood posted.

Mme Bouthiller – ex-teacher in a rural school, which means she probably went as far as the eighth grade herself – is a round, plump, ruddy little person in her early forties. She is what is known in these parts as a "grass widow", meaning that she is separated from her husband without, of course, being divorced. All this I learned from Mlle Placide (toys) the day after my arrival. I don't know whether Mme Bouthiller's husband sends her an allowance, but at all events she has a job as a clerk-receptionist with a photographer on Saint Onésime Avenue.

Mme Bouthiller has got into the habit of tapping on my door every Sunday morning about eleven to ask me whether I need anything and whether I am satisfied with my room. I invariably answer that I am perfectly satisfied, and on the whole this is the truth. The room is comfortable enough: the mattress is soft and there is lots of heat. The temperature runs to 78 or 80 degrees, which is no more than enough because my habit of sitting in the blast of Trefflé's hot-air register makes me a bit shivery anywhere else.

In appearance, on the other hand, my quarters are nothing fancy. The dusty rose paint is peeling off the walls in places and the greenish ceiling panels display several rather alarming cracks. The old armchair is covered in a threadbare cotton fabric. I sometimes entertain myself by pulling threads out of it at night after coming in from the beer parlour. Remarkably tough, those threads. I have a small dormer window that looks out over a rather squalid back yard littered with odd bits of old lumber and the rusty carcasses of two ancient trucks. No matter. The appearance of the external world has never meant much to me. Besides, this cotton-covered armchair has a new foam-rubber cushion which is very comfortable. I did lack a table to write on, but Mme Bouthiller got one for me the moment I asked her. This piece too is antediluvian, but if anything that is an advantage, for it means there is nothing to stop me from adding my own contribution to the innumerable scratches that scar its surface. On Sundays I often carve notches in the edge of it just to fill in time while trying to think of something to set down in this diary.

As I say, then, I have no complaints about my room. One enormous advantage it has is a separate entrance – by way of the junk-yard in the back, as a matter of fact. This way, I can come or go at any hour without bothering my hostess. It is especially handy at ten past one in the morning when I come in from Trefflé's. When I leave for work in the morning, about a quarter to nine, Mme Bouthiller is already gone anyway.

I am aware that these details are of no interest whatever. But no matter. The more words I write down, the more time I fill in. And how long a Sunday can be! Especially since I wake up on that day just as early as on any other; sometimes even a little earlier because the beer parlours close sharp at midnight on Saturdays.

Once my breakfast is disposed of (Bromo-Seltzer, Safe-All salts, tomato juice, and two bananas eaten in my room) I have nothing more to do. So I work on this diary. To think that it took four Sundays of nauseating boredom before this even occurred to me! But that part is over and there is no point in dwelling on it. So far this diary has fulfilled its function. I only hope it will go on doing so. My one fear is that I may find nothing to write about.

That is why I am in no great hurry to get rid of Mme Bouthiller when she knocks on my door about eleven o'clock upon her return from Mass. I won't say her visits delight me, but they don't annoy me. Besides, she never stays long because I never invite her to sit down. She stands leaning against the doorpost, one hip – the right one – more rounded than the other because of her posture, and her great bosom ballooning beneath her blouse. Of course I remain standing too. I don't see how I could do otherwise without offending her.

Our conversations invariably follow the same pattern. First the questions as to my domestic needs, to which I always reply that I don't need a thing. Then comes the remarks about the weather: Mme Bouthiller declares that it's chilly when it is cold, that it's windy when it is blowing, that it's snowy when we have had snow. I corroborate her observations and she proceeds to comment on the Mass she has just attended. It is at this point that the interrogation really gets under way. At the time of our first conversation I had not yet begun this diary, and my Sunday mornings were spent in wandering about the streets. Consequently Mme Bouthiller still didn't know whether I was attending Mass or not, so on that occasion she asked me what I thought of the Saint Joachim Church. I confessed that my powers of observation were not up to much and that I hesitated to pronounce judgment on any building without having seen it several dozen times. She wanted to know whether I had at least noticed the belfries, the highest in the county, it seems. I replied that while out walking I had sometimes caught a glimpse between buildings of these two tall, pointed steeples. She informed me that some people were of the opinion that the inside of the church was too dark. I drew her attention to the fact that this was not necessarily a fault; that many Roman-style churches were very dark, and that this didn't detract in any way from their beauty. They were different from the Gothic, that was all.

At this she changed the subject. Not that she had renounced

all further efforts to sound me out on my "convictions", but she no doubt considered that the conversation was taking an unfortunate tack.

Leaving the church, her investigations took on more scope, embracing the whole city. Did I find Saint Joachim tiny compared to the big city – from which no doubt I came? I answered that everything was relative, that I had indeed seen larger settlements than Saint Joachim, but that I had also seen smaller ones.

Then she wanted to know my views on whether the Joachimites had a peculiar way of speaking. I expressed the opinion that every town, indeed every little hamlet, possessed its own idiom and accent, but that the speech of Saint Joachim did not strike me as more strange than any other. A Frenchman might have been a bit thrown off, perhaps, but for myself I had no difficulty understanding. I added that I was not much of a judge in this area anyway, because I always paid the least possible attention to what people said to me. This remark had the effect of drying up her flow of words somewhat. After that she asked me only about a dozen more questions, to which, as I recall, my replies were suitably non-committal.

When it comes right down to it, I am not quite sure why I play hide-and-seek with her like this. There is plenty of information it wouldn't hurt me to give her. But no matter. I began this way and might as well keep it up. It is less tiring than trying to work out a new formula.

For her part, I think she has unraveled her whole life history to me with the exception of her relations with her husband. Of him she would say only that he was "a good-for-nothing, heartless ne'er-do-well, the worst kind of a heel, and the filthiest pig imaginable". She added that she conveyed this information to me out of a desire to be quite fair all round, and not for the purpose of giving me "a bad opinion" of him. As she seemed to be soliciting my approbation, I uttered a few words in praise of her respect for objective truth.

Next she began to talk of her two daughters, Angèle and Ursule, both married. Angèle lives in Lowell, Mass., and has two children, Frankie and Tom. Her husband is a little too fond of the bottle. Ursule lives in Farnham and is married to an army officer. They have no children, which is a great pity. Deep down, Mme Bouthiller suspects her son-in-law of impotency. He was wounded by a shell during the war. She has never been able to find out exactly where, which naturally justifies the worst suspicions. Mme Bouthiller sought my opinion on this point too. I expressed the view that artillery shells were indeed notorious for considering nothing sacred. This thought plunged my landlady into an abyss of meditation and there was a long silence.

Then, abruptly, she tackled the subject of her boss, a cadaverous old man of at least seventy. He is still given to the pursuit of petticoats and pinches the buttocks of his female employees whenever he gets a chance. Wasn't it shameful? At his age! Once again Mme Bouthiller demanded my opinion, so I gave it to her. I explained that to my way of thinking age had nothing to do with the matter. It was more a question of temperament. Mme Bouthiller objected that in that case M. Lesieur (for such is the name of her photographer) ought to tackle women his own age. While recognizing the logic of the argument, I advanced the hypothesis that for business reasons M. Lesieur was perhaps disinclined to fill his studio with septuagenarians, and that consequently he was compelled to confine his pinching activities to the ladies at hand. Mme Bouthiller appeared to find this irrefutable, and threw in the comment that in other respects M. Lesieur was a fine boss who had given her no real cause for complaint.

Then she left me. I have not given a complete account of our interview, obviously. That would take too long. Suffice it to say that she reported to me several other details, all no less fascinating. I may mention them later if I remember.

For the moment, however, let me get back to Léon's Book Shop where events have taken place recently which, given the monotony of my life, deserve to be considered important.

For the first few days after the conversation in the *sanctum sanctorum* nothing happened. Was the boss perhaps busy giving his "serious" readers confidential information to the effect that henceforth they could see me about their needs? I don't know. The only thing that surprised me was that M. Chicoine, after having so solemnly revealed to me the existence of his secret library, should now behave toward me as though nothing of significance had occurred. When I saw him he always seemed busy. Just time for a "Hello, how are you? Filthy weather, isn't it?" and he was gone.

One evening, however, he came in a little earlier than usual, took the money out of the cash register, deposited it in his little safe, and, on the stroke of five-thirty, managed to be at the front door just as I was leaving myself. Having inquired which way I was going, he declared that by a happy chance he was headed in the same direction himself. We walked a few steps in silence, then he suddenly said:

"You must have been surprised when you found your key wouldn't open the *sanctm sanctorum*, eh?"

He looked at me quizzically, his lips frozen in a hypocritical smile that bared his long equine teeth. But I was wary. I had already made myself sufficiently ridiculous with my oration on liberty, and I had no intention of letting down my guard a second time. So I informed him quite calmly that perhaps I might have been surprised had I had any occasion to use the key, but that as the issue had not arisen I had been able to preserve my equanimity. He looked a little let down at this, and felt impelled to offer an explanation.

"The thing is," he said, " – and I'm sorry about this – I lost my own key. The label said only '*sanctum sanctorum*', and there's nothing very compromising in that, I know; still I felt uncomfortable without that key because I'd never before let it out of my own hands. So a few days ago I decided it would be a good idea to replace the lock. I intended to mention it to you sooner, but as you know the ladies are always around the shop when I come in, and they don't miss a word I say."

The insincerity of this account smelled to high heaven. More than likely he had simply fallen into a fit of panic after giving me custody of these books which were "not for everyone's eyes". But whatever his real reasons, it was all the same to me. No answer seemed called for so I said nothing. No doubt he would have preferred more of a response, but as far as I was concerned he could damn well whistle for it, as the saying goes.

"That's why," he went on, stroking his chin, "I wanted to give you this other key, which fits the new padlock. I know you're a sensible fellow and I'm sure you'll use it with discretion."

I slipped the new key into my pocket and gave him back the old one. Then, finding ourselves in front of the snackbar where I usually gulp down a sandwich in the evening on my way to the beer parlour, I invited M. Chicoine to join me, making it quite clear at the same time that he could expect to pay for his own food. He assured me that nothing would give him greater pleasure, but that unfortunately he had another appointment, and we said good-night.

Eight or ten times in the following few days I had occasion to dig into the *sanctum sanctorum* for regular customers who were "serious purchasers". There is no problem to picking them out. They sidle up to me with a conspiratorial air and murmur into my ear the name of some author or book, all this in the tone of someone asking for a condom or a suppository in a drug store. Others are more evasive still: they shower me with meaningful glances and ask me to recommend "something a little out of the ordinary" or "something with a kick in it". Sometimes I say we have nothing of the sort, that our entire stock is right there on the shelves. A few have protested, and threatened to tell M. Léon about it. Others have let it go at that.

Why the refusals? The fact is that it irks me to have to go and root about in the *sanctum sanctorum*. If these jokers are just looking for an aphrodisiac, they can find more effective ones. I fail to see why I should put myself out when there are establishments in existence that specialize in the field. As far as I am concerned this is just not my job. Individual liberty? Freedom of thought? Fair enough. But that is not the issue here. If I had books "with a kick in them" conveniently to hand, I should be happy to pass them along to these characters if only to be rid of them. But there is a great deal more to it than that. Every trip to that accursed cellar – for that is what it is, underground or not – requires me to get up off my stool, walk round the corner, pass in front of Mlle Placide, open the door of an ice-cold back room, unlock the *sanctum sanctorum*, close the door behind me (the boss's orders are firm on that point), and feel my way about that dusty and ill-lit room looking for some book or other. If other customers happen to come in while I'm there – and of course whenever I leave my post they come running as though on a prearranged signal – Mlle Placide (toys) never fails to page me in strident tones. Since my refusal to help her with her displays, she would not lift her little finger to save me any trouble. Not that I blame her. All's fair in love and war. But the fact remains that whenever her yelping rings out I have to repeat in reverse all the operations described above, not to mention having to go all the way back to that same ice-box of a *sanctum sanctorum* later on.

It is not so bad when they ask for a specific title; a couple of minutes and I am back with the book. But when it comes to picking out some book "with a kick in it", I just won't go along. I have even had some customers leaf through the volume in question, announce that "it hasn't *enough* of a kick", and demand another. Needless to say, I send such characters packing – which, unfortunately, does not spare me the nuisance of having to return the book to the *sanctum sanctorum*.

It must be borne in mind that all this rushing about is supposed to take place without the other customers or the three old maids noticing anything! But let us get on.

One of my trips to the *sanctum sanctorum* has had some rather spectacular repercussions. Perhaps the word "spectacular" is excessive. Everything is relative, after all. It would be more accurate to say that the results have been upsetting for Léon's Book Shop in Saint Joachim, which is not exactly the hub of the universe.

It all began on a Thursday afternoon. This is a holiday at Saint Roch School, which is located a couple of miles from the town in open country, in the middle of a vast domain belonging to a community of clerics who combine the dairy industry with the rearing of young men. I had caught a glimpse of this school in the distance one Sunday (my third in Saint Joachim) when, for lack of something better to do, I had extended my walk as far as the city limits.

It is to be expected then that on Thursdays a certain number of high-school boys will come in and browse around the shop. A galling day, not because they practically never buy anything or because they poke fun at me – both matters of no importance – but because they shout their heads off, assail me with questions, and completely upset my arrangement of the shelves. After they leave, it takes me a good hour just to replace the books. All very natural at their age, I know, but that does not prevent me from being seized sometimes by an overwhelming urge to boot their backsides out the front door. But no matter.

So it was early one Thursday afternoon – one-thirty, perhaps two o'clock. Perched on my stool, my visor over my eyes, elbows on the counter, an open book in front of me, I was dozing as usual when a pimply-faced student wearing a beret came up to me and asked for the *Essay on Morals and Manners*. I raised my head to have a look at him. I should explain that I have trained myself not to appear startled when I am awakened like this. I found it was creating a bad impression. Thanks to my visor people now think I am reading. Mlle Placide is the only one who is not fooled. She has noticed that I never turn the pages of my book. What she does not know is that I never turn them even when I am awake. But no matter; all that is by the way. I was saying that I looked up at this high-school boy. I recognized him as one of the less noisy of the group. He often comes to the shop and spends hours leafing through uncut volumes. I was like that at his age, an omnivorous reader. I could not begin to estimate how many bits and pieces of "recent releases" I have read in my time in this fragmentary fashion. When he asked me for the *Essay* my first impulse was to refuse, to tell him we didn't have it. After all, selling Voltaire to a kid his age could get me into hot water. Then I thought better of it. Was it mere curiosity, or a kind of fellow-feeling produced by nostalgia for my own school-days? However that may be, I asked him for the name of the author as though I didn't know myself, and he told me. I asked whether the work was a sociological study. He looked at me with great condescension and explained that it was a book of historical interpretation. To all appearances he took me for a complete numbskull. But no matter: he knew what he wanted, at least. I don't doubt that he was more of a "serious" purchaser than many others to whom I had previously sold *sanctum sanctorum* books. All the same I was momentarily tempted to warn him that, besides being an expensive volume, the *Essay on Morals and Manners* is about as dull a book as you could hope to find. But what was the use? Young fellows of that age are suspicious of their elders. He would immediately have taken it into his head that I was trying to keep him away from "dangerous reading". Much better for him to find out for himself. So I went and got the book and gave it to him. He looked at it for a moment in apparent unbelief, then picked it up, paid me, and made off as fast as his legs could carry him.

For the next three or four days I heard nothing more about it. My routine went on as usual – book shop, beer parlour, room; room, book shop, beer parlour. I suppose in this period I sold another dozen or so volumes from the *sanctum sanctorum*. . . .

Then, one morning, in came the parish priest. I knew who he was right away because the three old maids called him *"Monsieur le curé"*. As far as I knew, it was the first time he had set foot in our establishment. I had supposed he just wasn't much of a reader – unless he was keeping himself supplied with books through other channels. Father Bonet is a corpulent man on the near side of sixty and very well preserved, with a ruddy complexion, a flat nose, a receding forehead, a great bush of hair, a solemn drawling voice. He came up to me and asked in a whisper whether I was "in charge of books". From all appearances he did not want the ladies to overhear our conversation. I recall that at that moment a dead silence reigned in the shop, so I answered very distinctly that except for Friday evenings, when M. Chicoine was there himself, and the noon hour, when Mlle Morin took over for me, I was indeed in charge of the book department, as my presence behind the counter indicated.

He thanked me with a nod and began to examine the display of books. He even asked to borrow a little step-stool so that he could reach the volumes on the upper shelves. From time to time he compared some of the titles with a list taken from his pocket, and shook his head. I left him to his own devices. Seated on my stool, I eventually succeeded in dozing off as usual. In a little while he came down again and asked in the same confidential tone as before whether we didn't have in stock "certain dangerous books". Raising my eyebrows to give myself an air of perplexity, I asked to be enlightened on what was meant by "dangerous books". His voice betrayed some impatience:

"Come now, you know quite well what I mean. Books that are not for everybody's eyes."

I replied that I knew nothing about such things. I was not much of a reader myself, I explained, and even if I had been, I would scarcely take it upon myself to pass judgment on such matters. He stared at me motionlessly for a few seconds. I expect he was wondering whether I was as stupid as I appeared.

"Have you no reference work giving the moral rating of the books you sell?" he inquired.

I told him I knew nothing about that either but that if he would give me the title of this reference book I would consult our lists. He named Sagehomme and Bethléem.

I knew quite well we did not have these authors. Nevertheless, I put on an air of great concentration and spent several minutes consulting the lists before answering that we did not stock them. At the same time I assured him that if he wanted these volumes we could certainly order them for him. He would have them in about ten days.

42

He frowned and subjected me to another long scrutiny. Then, abruptly, he drew a book from the inside pocket of his overcoat and thrust it under my nose.

"Are you familiar with this volume?" His voice was severe.

It was the *Essay on Morals*. I told him I could not recall, but that it did seem to me I had seen the name of the author somewhere.

"Then this book didn't come from this shop?"

I took the *Essay* in my hands, examined the front and back covers, looked inside, and gave it back to the curate with the remark that I did not think it came from our shop, inasmuch as our books had our name in them on a little sticker attached to the inside of the cover. I showed him what I meant by reference to another volume. I added that of course this tab might have come unstuck, in fact I had noticed that the latest batch of stickers did not seem to adhere too well. However, not being able to make out the slightest mark or trace of glue in the book he had shown me, I was strongly inclined to think it had not come from our shop.

Father Bonet stood motionless for some time, scratching his chin in puzzlement. Once or twice he opened his mouth, but each time closed it again without saying anything. Finally he slipped the book back into the pocket of his coat and thanked me for the information.

I assured him that I was entirely at his service and asked him whether he wanted me to order the two volumes he had mentioned by Bethléem and Sagehomme. He needed a few seconds to take this in, because he was thinking of something else. Finally he answered no, he already had the books at the presbytery: he had simply wanted to consult them on the spot. I then asked whether I could not interest him in some other books. As he had been able to observe, we kept quite a full stock, and it would be an honour to serve him. This was the first time I had ever pushed a sale. I was rather hoping to unload one of the white elephants on him. But it failed to come off. I am not really much of a salesman. The priest bowed out on the grounds of poor eyesight. Having noticed that he read without glasses, I took the liberty of expressing some surprise, and advanced the hypothesis that perhaps he had only meant to say that his eyes tired quickly. He said yes, this was indeed precisely what he had meant. I then hastened to congratulate him upon enjoying such good vision at an age when most people can hardly see at all. As previously mentioned, he cannot be over sixty and my compliment left him unmoved. He cleared his throat noisily, adjusted his scarf, and took his leave with a very frigid "Good-day".

During this exchange I had kept quite calm, and, if I may say so, had shown considerable presence of mind. But the moment the priest was out the door a strange exultation overcame me. I had to turn my back to the counter and pretend to be busy replacing books in order to conceal my emotion from the eyes of the old maids. I cannot be sure I succeeded. I know my gestures were abrupt and jerky, quite different from my normal languid manner. If Father Bonet had returned at that moment I should have been incapable of repeating my feat of a few moments before. For feat it was, no getting away from that. All things considered, I had won a little victory, and this, as indicated, without any open quarrel or the slightest sign of ill-will. Fortunately none of the ladies chose that moment to come and talk to me. But I could hear them whispering among themselves, their mutual hostility momentarily suspended by the circumstances.

The rest of the day passed off without incident. I served some customers, gave evasive answers to others. Mlle Morin replaced me at lunch time. The afternoon was rather quiet until about five o'clock, when a whining, cantankerous old shrew pulled about twenty volumes from the shelves and strewed them about the counter without buying a single one. I pointed out to her that the practice was well established among our customers of putting back books they took off the shelves. She retorted that nobody with any bringing up at all would make such a remark to an old woman of her age, who was crippled with rheumatism to the point where every move meant excruciating pain. I replied in turn that if such was the case an excellent way to spare herself this agony would have been to extract fewer books from the shelves, or better still, to stay at home in the first place. This perfectly reasonable piece of advice failed to please her. She took off, muttering imprecations on the decline of good manners in our part of the country.

Shortly after, M. Chicoine came in as usual. He emptied the cash-drawers and the three old maids left the shop. I hung around while the boss went over the day's receipts and entered them in the ledger. I had several other books to restore to the shelves besides the ones pulled out by the old harpy. To be quite candid, my department looked like an old bird-cage. M. Chicoine made no remarks, but when he had finished with his accounts he came over to my counter and stood watching me work. I wondered whether he had already heard about the visit from the priest. I'm sure my manner was still a bit feverish. The silence stretched out to the point of embarrassment. For the sake of having something to say I asked M. Chicoine whether there were any brothels in Saint Joachim. Now that I think of it the subject was rather well chosen, because it might suggest to him an explanation for my unusual mannerisms and draw him down a false trail – which is exactly what happened. My question immediately brought a broad smile to his horsy features. His upper lip rose to reveal long yellowish teeth and a good portion of the gums. I could not help thinking that he looked a lot like Fernandel. But he was as

45

obliging as could be. He informed me that unfortunately such establishments did not exist in Saint Joachim. Rather a nuisance he agreed – "for those who need them, of course", and here his eyebrows rose enigmatically. There had formerly been one, "definitely first-class, too", and it had done a very good business. But it had had to close its doors because of "certain pressures brought to bear". Interested parties now had to go to Saint Jules, "a larger city and, according to some, more responsive to the needs of modern society". For himself, M. Chicoine would make no judgment on this point. A Joachimite from way back, he refused to run down his own city. Besides, I must understand that he was a great believer not only in individual freedom but in collective freedom as well. Was I not of his opinion? I reassured him on this point, but not without pointing out that these two kinds of freedom were often at odds; that in many cases the majority which expressed the general or "official" view was composed of individuals so plagued and buffeted by fear – by "pressures brought to bear", as he had put it – that their so-called collective freedom represented nothing more than the sum total of their individual servitudes. M. Chicoine burst into paeans of praise for this labyrinthine analysis, which, he declared, expressed his own thoughts on the subject better than he could himself. I wondered idly whether it was in Jean-Jacques Rousseau or somewhere else that I had picked up this "analysis" of mine. Scraps of former reading sometimes bob into my memory like that. But I was given no time to reflect further on the matter. M. Chicoine was already telling me that one of his friends went fairly regularly to Saint Jules by car, and that he was sure he would be glad to take me along. I thanked him but declined the offer with the remark that I hated moving about, even for short distances, and that anyway there was nothing urgent about it. Besides, it occurred to me to add, perhaps with a little scouting about I might find what I wanted right here in town.

46

April 14

The day of the pastoral visit had exhausted me and for some reason the prospect of my usual evening at Trefflé's nauseated me. Perhaps I was feeling the need to talk to someone. Anything is possible. At Trefflé's my habits are so solidly established, and recognized by all, that I could not expect to strike up a friendly conversation there. Who with, anyway? Old Man Manseau? What could we two possibly have to talk about? For him, I expect those grunted salutations represent the very pinnacle of sociability.

As there was nothing doing in that direction, I decided to get myself a quick bite to eat and then buy a bottle of rum and go back to my room. Maybe Mme Bouthiller would be at home. After all I knew practically nothing of her habits. Except for M. Chicoine, she was the only person in Saint Joachim with whom I had ever held anything approaching a long conversation. In Montreal, when seized with a fit of sociability (which happened perhaps twice a year), I could always go and plague my old schoolmates.

As I had hoped, Mme Bouthiller was at home. I caught sight of her through the kitchen window doing the dishes. I went rapidly up to my room and tossed down a good shot of rum to screw up my courage. I remember standing before my dresser mirror and adjusting the knot of my tie. Perhaps I was already a bit tipsy. The reflected image was not particularly encouraging. I gulped down another shot of rum and went downstairs. I must have been upstairs longer than I thought. The dishes were done and put away. Mme Bouthiller was sitting at the kitchen table sipping coffee. She had evidently heard me coming down, for she was sitting motionless, the cup poised in her two hands, her elbows leaning on the oil-cloth. She was the first to speak:

"Well, to what do I owe the pleasure? This isn't rent day!" (I usually give her my six dollars on Sundays when she stops by my room.)

I greeted her rather ceremoniously and told her that this was not a business call. I had seen the announcement of a good film at the Palace theatre and I wanted to invite her to go with me....

She looked at me in wide-eyed surprise. Nothing in my demeanour up to that time had prepared her for such a move as this. I went on to say that it was no fun going to the movies alone: when there was an interesting bit in the film you had no one to talk it over with, and it made it all rather dull.... I have no idea whether my words were well chosen. Besides, in situations like this, words count for very little. If a woman is going to accept, the language of the invitation makes no difference; and if she intends to refuse you're wasting your breath anyway.

"Frankly, Monsieur Jodoin, the idea appeals to me," she

said, "only you know what it's like in a small town. People would talk...."

I put it to her that you could never get away from silly chatter anywhere and that the only way to treat it was with complete contempt. Mme Bouthiller agreed with me in theory, but hesitated to do so in practice. If I had "gone through what she had" I should be more sensitive to what people might say. Monsieur Bouthiller was, to be sure, "a good-for-nothing, heartless ne'er-do-well, the worst kind of a heel, and the filthiest pig imaginable", and yet at the time of the separation there had been poisonous tongues ready to stick up for him. ...The conversation was going sour, and I was mentally resigning myself to an evening of solitary tippling in my own room when I hit on a device that saved the situation. I suggested that we should each make our way separately to the Palace theatre and meet inside as though by chance. In the darkness people would not recognize us, and anyway a chance encounter could not possibly give rise to any gossip. This last argument did the trick. Deep down, I think she was anxious to accept anyway. But no matter: we followed my plan and had no difficulty finding each other in the orchestra seats.

I scarcely looked at the films. As was to be expected, one of them was a Western: fist-fights, gun-fights, galloping in the dust, Machiavellian plots, cattle-rustlng, the eventual triumph of the bow-legged, iron-jawed Romeo who, at the end of the film, takes in his arms a freckle-faced Juliet. The other film may have been set in the West Indies, or perhaps in some Pacific island. I cannot quite remember whether the natives inserted Spanish exclamations into their dialogue. As for Mme Bouthiller, she followed no better than I did, for she doesn't understand English. But, as she remarked, "as long as it moves, that's the main thing". I expect I dozed off for short periods.

About the middle of the show I nonchalantly took her hand. The palm was rough, like that of a laundress. This surprised me at the time, but I have learned since that, besides greeting the customers at the establishment of her seventy-year-old bottom-pinching photographer, Mme Bouthiller also does some of the film-developing. Anyway, this roughness put me off a little. But as she abandoned her hand to me without resistance, it would have been improper for me to withdraw my own. So we held hands until the end of the performance – or rather until a few mintes before the end, for Mme Bouthiller, perfecting my strategy, had thought it wiser for us to leave separately and meet once more "by chance" in the vestibule.

So I got up first to go out and wait for her, as had been agreed. By this time my little adventure was beginning to rub me the wrong way. Moreover, I was thirsty. As previously mentioned, I had had only two shots of rum before leaving the house, and that was three and a half hours before. Healthy as those shots may have been, they were no substitute for the fifteen or twenty glasses of beer I was used to drinking each evening at Trefflé's.

Walking home, with a sharp wind penetrating my thread-bare old overcoat, I was inwardly cursing the whole project. I told myself that I should have been further ahead to go to Trefflé's as usual. Now it was too late. I consoled myself with the thought that my bottle of rum was still three-quarters full. With that, I could always get by.

Back at the house, I committed what was perhaps another boner. I say "perhaps" because the point is debatable: it is too recent for me to be able to judge it objectively. Once inside the house, I proposed a drink to warm us up. So far as I was concerned this was more of a polite gesture than anything else, for I was inclined to expect a refusal. Her half-spoken queries about my religious habits had given me the impression that Mme Bouthiller was perhaps sternly pious. True, she was not living with her husband, but in cases like that women can usually find some "honourable" reason. But no matter.

She accepted my invitation with the remark that it was a bit cold at that. Furthermore, not being familiar with rum, she was rather curious to taste it. The bottle was in my pocket, but I pretended to have left it upstairs so as to have an excuse to go and gulp down a good swig on my own, for I was thirsty.

I came back down and we sat down on the love-seat in the living-room. There is no point in going into the details. They are of no interest. We drank four or five small glasses together. Mme Bouthiller had perhaps never tasted rum, but she was certainly not a total stranger to strong drink. I must say she held her liquor admirably, in spite of her repeated declarations that each glass must be her last, that we must be reasonable, that she had to get up early the next day, and so on. As for myself, I was beginning to feel quite at home. I agreed with everything she said and kept pouring.

After the fifth or sixth glass I took her hand again, rough as it was, and gently started to feel around. The speed of her reaction was surprising, not to say a little embarrassing, because I was not feeling entirely ready myself. But everything worked out nicely. I simply dragged out a little the business of undressing her. She herself evidently grasped the situation, for she did what was necessary with effectiveness if not with refinement. Besides, I am far from being a connoisseur. My sex-life has never been immoderate. It is too tiring. But no matter. The point is that I spent a pleasant night with Rose – for such is her Christian name. The next day, naturally enough, I felt a bit limp. But she served me a good breakfast – ham and eggs, marmalade, coffee, etc. – and on the whole I was quite satisfied.

April 28

It has been two weeks since I touched this diary. I am writing these lines in the waiting-room of the Saint Joachim railway station, located at the eastern edge of the city, half an hour's walk from my room. I say "my" room only out of habit, for it hardly belongs to me any more. True, I still pay the rent, and consequently must be considered the tenant, but since our night out at the movies, Rose thinks she has the right to enter it at any hour of the night or day. At night I don't much care. I always come in half lit and half asleep. Whether Rose is in my bed or not, it is all the same to me. She doesn't snore or kick. I go to sleep almost instantly with the warmth of her body near my own, which is not unpleasant. But during the day – I mean on Sundays, for I am never there any other day – the situation becomes intolerable; so bad, in fact, that it almost makes me forget the confounded mess at the book store.

But let us not mix the two departments. Let us proceed in order. First of all my love-life – if you can call it that. Then the *sanctum sanctorum*.

As I've already indicated, the little love-frolic that followed our night out at the movies had not been unpleasant. Of course I am not as young as I used to be and I no longer have the verve of yesteryear, which in my case had never been spectacular anyway. But no matter; on the whole I was pleased with myself. I had proved that I was still more or less virile. I know this is not an unusual talent, but it is something. At the same time I was not anxious to repeat the experiment – at least not for a while. So I was disagreeably surprised early the following Sunday morning, while I was still in bed, to see Rose come into my room. She was dressed informally, as the saying goes: a filmy dressing-gown of flowered green, which she proceeded to remove as she slipped in beside me under the covers. In a way it was rather nice. I do not deny it. I am not completely uncivilized. But I was scarcely awake; I had my usual morning headache, and I was in no mood for fun and games. How could I explain that to Rose? I had not seen her since the evening of our movie. I will say in her favour that she had kept her distance. No doubt she was waiting for me to make the first move – or rather the second first move. Probably I ought to have gone downstairs to see her once or twice during the week, if only for a little petting. Maybe that would have satisfied her. But how is a man to know? You cannot ask a woman that sort of thing – though, come to think of it, I don't see why. But no matter. If a person were to try to find reasons for everything in life there would be no end to it.

Anyway, last Sunday Rose came into my room in the flowered dressing-gown, took it off, and slipped in beside me. After that it was up to me to rise to the occasion. At first I thought I couldn't. My head was throbbing and I had had no chance to take my Safe-All salts. On top of that, I discovered that Rose had a cushion of fat, a kind of spare tire, in the region of the midriff. Much as I told myself it did not matter, my mind refused to leave it alone. And yet I am no more fastidious than the next man. I know I am far from perfect myself. My face speaks for itself: long and limp, with two creases that look like parentheses linking the nostrils to the corners of the mouth. Add to that a pair of bushy eyebrows, joined together and rising to a point over the nose, and two ears that stick out from the head at right angles. Only the eyes are any good at all. I have even been told that they are handsome. But no matter; this really has nothing to do with the case. I do not know whether Rose considers me ugly. She has never mentioned the subject and of course I have never asked her. The point is that nobody with my looks has any right to get finicky about a little fat round the middle. But I just could not help it. It fascinated me. To get my mind onto something else I started to talk about the films we had been to see together. Rose must have been a bit taken aback by this, but she managed to reply in a fairly natural tone. She is not entirely lacking in tact. After that, what with one thing and another, I forgot about the spare tire and was able to perform. It was a pleasant surprise. I am not so far gone after all.

If Rose had then left me to myself after a decent interval, I should have had no complaint. But two hours later she was still there hashing over her past life, with whose dreary vicissitudes I was already all too familiar from our previous conversations. I broached the subject of breakfast and declared that my stomach was growling with hunger. She hastened to apologize and practically drove me downstairs into the dining-room. Naturally I could not eat and run, so we went on talking, and somehow, without my noticing it, it was not long before Rose had started fixing dinner. Once more there was no escape. To make a long story short, we spent the day together. By evening I was in a savage mood, which I blamed on the headache. She was full of solicitude and offered to call the doctor. I begged off with the remark that a good night's sleep would put me back on my feet.

Twice, in the course of the following week, she came back at one in the morning just as I was getting in from Trefflé's. Fortunately I had foreseen the possibility of just such an eventuality and had drunk a few extra glasses, so I was able to drop off to sleep the moment my head touched the pillow.

But I swore that this Sunday would not be like the last. I set my alarm for seven, got up, and left the house. I had planned to get settled right here in the station immediately after breakfast, but the building does not open until nine-thirty on Sunday. There are only two trains that day: one at 10:10 in the morning and the other at 4:30 p.m. Having tried the station door to no avail, I strolled off toward the river. The walk along the banks is quite pleasant. A cement sidewalk bordered by poplars stretches in both directions from the swing-bridge. About half way along there is a bandstand, and if the weather had been different I should have considered spending the day there. But this was out of the question in a temperature of thirty to thirty-five degrees. So I wandered along the banks until about nine-fifteen and at exactly nine-thirty I was waiting at the station door. The stationmaster came along a few moments later. We nodded at each other and he examined me from head to foot, after which he announced that the train would be a good half-hour late.

"You understand?" he persisted, seeing that I failed to react.

I told him I understood perfectly well, then came and sat down on this bench next to the radiator which is hissing and spitting in the corner where I am writing these lines. In accordance with the stationmaster's announcement, the train showed up at about ten-forty. There were a few of the local sods hanging around the waiting-room, among others a family of five, including a snotty little brat who howled without respite.

They left at last and I was alone in my corner, secure in the prospect of unbroken peace and quiet at least until four-thirty in the afternoon. But my unorthodox procedures, and the sheets of paper I was juggling on my knee, had caught the interest of the stationmaster, and were perhaps worrying him. He came over and asked what train I was waiting for. I answered that I was not waiting for a train at all – that in fact I was delighted to learn there were only two. Looking more and more suspicious, he wanted to know whether I lived in Saint Joachim. It was obviously better to satisfy his curiosity once and for all; otherwise he would pester me the whole day, or possibly even call the police, who knows? So I told him that I had been living in Saint Joachim for six weeks, that I worked at Léon's Book Shop on Fourteenth Street, that I roomed at Mme Bouthiller's on Eighth Street, that I often dropped in to Trefflé's beer parlour. At the mention of Trefflé's, a broad grin opened beneath the moustache that adorned the porcine countenance of the stationmaster.

"Ah, it's you?" he exclaimed, delighted with his discovery. "You're the one! Some of my friends have told me about you...."

His words made it clear to me that, in spite of my quiet, regular habits, I enjoyed a substantial reputation in Saint Joachim. The stationmaster was contemplating me with an amused twinkle in his eyes, as though I were an irresistible clown. I could see I had won the toss already, but to flatter his sense of authority I told him I had no intention of breaking any of the rules of the C.N.R. It was just that I liked stations, I explained: they had an agreeable atmosphere, at once intimate and impersonal. I told him I envied him for being able to spend his days in such a place, and that I wished only to sit there and write a few letters to dear and distant friends. Porky immediately assumed a protective air and put his hand on my shoulder.

"You can stay here as long as you like," he declared, thrusting out his chest. "Only thing I can't let you do is lie down on the benches. That's forbidden. The inspectors don't come round often, but if they ever caught you stretched out on a bench while I'm around, it would be tough on me, catch on?"

I assured him I had no desire to lie down, inasmuch as I had had a good night's rest and could always go back to my room if I got sleepy.

He retreated behind his grill with an air of satisfaction. I am sure that by tomorrow half the town will know that I have spent the day here on a bench in the C.N.R. waiting-room. I couldn't care less. The fact remains that if I had not been able to persuade old Porky to let me stay here I should have had to think about getting another room, and I hate moving.

May 5

I am again able to write in my room –
for today at least. When I came in last night, or rather early this
morning, I found a note on my dressing-table. It was from
Rose telling me that she would be away today. A trip to
Farnham. Would I please put my rent money on the living-
room table? Nothing more. A rather cool communication.
Rose is offended, it appears. Who cares? She has not tried to
see me again since last Sunday. No doubt she heard about my
day in the station. Naturally she was hurt. It was a pretty
clear indication that she was becoming a nuisance. There was
nothing else to do. Had I been able to think of a gentler method
of making the break I should have used it. All in all, I have
nothing against Rose. She is a bit of a pest, which is not her
fault; I am not very active sexually, which is not mine. . . . But

enough of that. I have other nuts to crack, for while the situation is improving in the love-life department, down at the shop things are getting sticky.

Monday afternoon, when M. Chicoine tore past my counter, his eye haggard, his hair unkempt, his face livid, and when, without so much as a word of greeting, he dived into his office, I knew immediately that something nasty was in the wind. Naturally I didn't budge from my stool. The boss had stomped through the shop without a word to anybody, and I am sure his rudeness offended the old maids more than it did me. Though they almost never speak to each other, I could hear them now cackling away around the stationery counter. I could even catch sight of them, thanks to the little holes in the upper edge of my visor. They kept turning their eyes in my direction. I knew I had only to raise my head to be bombarded with questions. Perhaps they would have started in on me anyway, in spite of my somnolent appearance, if M. Chicoine had given them time. But hardly two minutes passed before he sprang out of his office as tempestuously as he had dashed in. He ordered me rudely into the back room, and immediately slammed the door again behind him. There followed a few seconds of complete silence. I made no move. The old maids, frozen into attitudes of stunned amazement, stared at my motionless form bent over the counter. The hinges of the office door squeaked again. Half choked with rage, M. Chicoine shouted:

"Are you deaf? Don't you understand when you're spoken to?"

When I raised my head and looked at him I thought for one moment that he was actually going to make for me. Instinctively I grasped the long pole with the adjustable fork on the end, which I use to pull books from the upper shelves. I don't think anyone saw my gesture because this pole is slung horizontally on two hooks behind the counter. But there was no need to use it, and I am now inclined to think that my fear was groundless. Anyway, I replied very slowly and calmly that I had understood perfectly the sense of his vociferations, and that if I had not complied it was because, subordinate though I might be, I did not own that this gave him the right to insult me, especially in the presence of the ladies.

This reply produced a remarkable effect on M. Chicoine. He opened and closed his mouth several times, passing his hand repeatedly over his waxy forehead, before snapping at the old maids that they could leave. They took as long as possible to get into their coats, but finally, noticing the severe eye of M. Chicoine upon their every gesture, they disappeared.

As soon as the door had closed on the last of them the boss turned upon me once again. The quiet restraint of his voice seemed all the more menacing by contrast with the outbursts of a moment before.

"Perhaps you think," he hissed, "that you can claim a secure position because you've succeeded in worming out of me the secret of the *sanctum sanctorum*? Well, you're wrong! I'm the boss around here and I intend to remain so."

It seemed futile to point out the gross inaccuracy of this statement. I contented myself with the remark that I made no claim to anything, except to the kind of treatment that was consistent with respect for my freedom as an individual. I admit that this did not mean much, but he had so filled my ears with his chatter about freedom, that my reply took some of the wind out of his sails. He muttered something about people who always want to bandy words, and then, after a few moments devoted to striding up and down the room and biting his lip, he planted himself before me and announced in the voice of a tragedian:

"Father Bonet came to see me at my house today."

Nothing in this bulletin seemed to call for comment, so I awaited the sequel in silence.

"Do you understand what I'm telling you?" he hissed between clenched teeth.

I reassured him on this point, stating that, if I were not mistaken, a fairly average intelligence could grasp the sense of an announcement such as this. He peered at me quizzically, appearing to hesitate between fury and pity. Perhaps the priest had convinced him that when it came to brains I was not up to much.

"Do you know *why* he came to see me?"

I pointed out that, being unfamiliar with the nature of his relations with the priest, I felt myself to be in a poor position to formulate any hypothesis on the subject. His reply came like the crack of a whip. It was absolutely ear-splitting and decidedly unpleasant.

"Why didn't you tell me about his visit here last Friday, you miserable son of a..."

Without waiting to hear precisely which aspect of my genealogy he felt most appropriate to the situation, I cut in to retort that if I had not mentioned the priest's call it was because, to the best of my knowledge, I had been able to answer all the questions he had put to me. I added that in my opinion a good employee should not bother his employer except in spheres beyond his own competence. If, I went on, the priest had wanted to order books that we did not have in stock, then I would certainly have referred the matter to him, M. Chicoine, knowing that he always took personal charge of orders of this kind. Once more he looked at me in bewilderment. Then, suddenly, he slapped onto the desk a copy of the *Essay on Morals*.

"Did you sell this book to a young student?"

I picked up the book, turned it over in my hands, flipped through the pages, and then stated that, although I was in no position to assert positively that this book was the one I had sold to a pimply young man in a green beret who did indeed look as though he might be a student, the thing was not beyond the bounds of possibility.

At this, M. Chicoine smote his receding forehead with the palm of his hand.

"So, you have the nerve to admit it!"

In my reply I emphasized that I had not in fact admitted anything at all, but that, even if I had, I didn't see that in so doing I had displayed any particular nerve.

Judging by his facial contortions, this reply gave M. Chicoine something of a jolt, as the saying has it. For several seconds I had the odd impression that he was going to explode, literally, and actually fly to pieces like a grenade. But he eventually regained control, and his voice was almost plaintive as he resumed:

"Can you tell me... can you explain to me what in God's name possessed you to sell such a book to a young student? You see: I'm entirely calm. I'm really trying to understand. Now, why?"

Before dealing directly with this question, I took occasion to remind him that he himself, M. Chicoine, had of his own free will revealed to me the existence of the *sanctum sanctorum*, and that I had consequently presumed, perhaps wrongly, that I was authorized to sell books from it, while using, of course, a certain amount of discretion...

"But to a student, for Christ's sake! And you talk of discretion! You have the gall to talk of discretion!"

I pointed out that, when we had discussed the matter previously, no mention had been made of social classes or professions. I remembered quite precisely. Consequently the matter of students had never come up. The whole question had been confined to "serious" readers. To my way of looking at it, a serious reader was one who reads conscientiously the books he buys, not just to kill time or to look for obscenities, but to search for ideas, theories, criticisms, all these perhaps contrary to his own view of things, but capable of making him think. It struck me that students fell very precisely into this category. As for Voltaire's soporific *Essay*, I agreed that it was no doubt ill-chosen to produce the effect I was describing. But that was only a personal opinion. The student had asked me for the book. I had sold it to him. It was up to him to decide. I added that, if Voltaire's critics, by the very violence of their disparagements and prohibitions, had not succeeded in inflating his reputation beyond all measure, it would perhaps never have occurred to the student to read him; or, if he did read him, he would observe, if he had any intelligence, how superficial and out of date were most of the ideas of the aforementioned Voltaire, with the exception of his pleas for tolerance....

I stopped, surprised to have said so much. My tirade sounded straight out of the lecture hall. As for M. Chicoine, he was bathed in sweat.

"I hope you didn't expound these...theories to Father Bonet," he asked, almost plaintively.

I reassured him: between the priest and myself there had been no question of any theories. He uttered a sigh of relief.

"Well, then, what did happen exactly?"

I described the scene of the previous Friday as closely as I remembered it.

"You're not forgetting anything?"

I told him no.

M. Chicoine resumed his pacing of the room. When he came to a halt, he brought forth his bottle of Scotch and offered me a glass, which I accepted without comment. We drank wordlessly. It was he who broke the silence:

"Do you know that Father Bonet thinks you're...queer?"

He was watching me out of the corner of his eye. I inquired whether the word "queer" was a figure of speech in the present context, whether it stood for "moronic" or even "idiotic". The boss gestured theatrically:

"Now let's not make a mountain out of a mole-hill. All I said was ...queer."

I thanked him for the clarification and declared that everyone had a right to his opinion, but that the parish priest had no special competence in this field.

M. Chicoine agreed profusely, and added that anyway the question was of no importance. I didn't exactly share his view on that, but I saw no point in interrupting him. According to him, what was "crucial" for the moment was that the priest should have no proof that the *Essay on Morals* had come from Léon's Book Shop.

"I must admit too that you threw him off the track completely. Right now at Saint Roch School, everybody is more or less convinced that the young fellow got the book in some other way that he doesn't want to reveal to the principal. You know those young jokers: they have their own peculiar code of honour. So, if the priest comes back, just act innocent."

I made bold to remark that I did not find M. Chicoine's expression a happy one. If what he meant by "innocent" was "stupid" then I demurred. If, on the other hand, he was using it as the antonym of "guilty", then I considered it inappropriate, inasmuch as I felt in no way blameworthy. He put his hand on my shoulder and assured me that he felt the same way about it. To prove that he meant what he said he was going to retain me in his employ "whatever the pressures brought to bear". If he expected me to show graditude, he must have been disappointed. I knew full well that if M. Chicoine was "retaining" me, for the moment, it was not out of philanthropy or regard for me, and that a few polite words would not alter the situation one way or the other.

So I took my leave with a mere good-bye.

My appearance at Trefflé's three-quarters of an hour later caused something of a sensation. Ordinarily the other drinkers scarcely notice me. An identifying glance, nothing more. Usually the only greeting I get is from Old Man Manseau, who touches two fingers to the peak of his cap. But on this particular evening all eyes were fixed upon me. There was much whispering, elbow-nudging, and snickering. None of these manoeuvres affected me in the slightest.

I reached my table in the corner near the hot-air vent. Joe came and put my two glasses in front of me as usual and, again as usual, I gave him a quarter. He thanked me and put the coin in his pocket. But instead of moving off right away, he began to wipe a nearby table, which was perfectly dry, and to move chairs about with aimless little gestures. Finally he tackled the subject that was on his mind:

"Seems business is pretty good at the book shop these days?"

I could not suppress a little pucker of annoyance. Hitherto people had left me alone in the beer parour. Was I now to be plagued with questions? I informed the waiter that as far as I knew the balance sheet indicated a satisfactory turnover.

Joe continued to scrub the faultless enamel surface of the little metal table. He resumed with a conspiratorial wink:

"Those books of yours, now, seems some of 'em ain't exactly moth-eaten, from what I hear?"

This question made everything clear to me: the whole town was aware of my encounter with the parish priest. I answered curtly that I could not attest to the meaning of the expression "moth-eaten", but that we sold books of several different kinds.

This reply appeared to strike him as uproariously funny. He burst into a guffaw and the eyes of the whole room converged on my table.

"Different books! Different! You said it! That's a hot one, that is!"

As his giggling subsided he bent over me and began to murmur into my ear:

"Look, I been talkin' to a couple of the boys here, pals of mine, you know. Couldn't you fix it up to slip them a couple of your books?... They're ready to pay, don't worry about that. These guys don't mind kickin' through with five bucks if they have to, or even ten...."

I told him stiffly that if these gentlemen would be so good as to call at the shop and give me the titles in which they were interested I should be happy to serve them – provided, of course, that we had the volumes in stock.

"That's not it at all," said Joe. "You know what I mean: somethin' about morals; you know the sort of stuff. You don't need to worry: with me mum's the word, you know that. Same for the others. They're not wet behind the ears either. You just tuck the stuff under your coat and bring it here. We'll slip you the dough, and mum's the word. Catch on?"

So even the title of the book I had sold the student was common knowledge around town, and the mere word "morals" had been enough to launch the good Joachimites into a frenzy of erotic rhapsodies. This was getting serious. Nonsense like this about my books could very well increase my trade and, with it, the number of trips to the *sanctum sanctorum*. Such a threat had to be strangled at birth.

I made it clear to Joe that I was not employed at Léon's Book Shop as a messenger boy. If his friends wanted some books "of a special kind", they had better apply to a larger establishment than ours. And finally, I told him, I flatly refused to transact business here in the beer parlour.

"Yeah!"

Joe tossed his head in disappointment, but I could see that he was mainly impressed by my caution. Let us hope that he has been rebuffed permanently. I watched him move about from one table to the other passing on my reply.

After that I settled down to drink as usual. Nobody spoke to me until about twelve-thirty. Then Old Man Manseau, who had held himself imperturbably apart from the discussion until now, struggled painfully onto his rheumatic legs and made his way to my table. His bronzed, expressionless face was an inch from my ear.

"I heerd about this here set-to," he said. "Now 'tain't none o' my business, but yer a new feller 'round here. Me, I bin draggin' my carcass 'round these parts for more'n sixty years, and I seen a thing or two. Well, lemme tell ya, 'tain't good for the health 'round here to go agin the priests. In these parts they're the boys with the pull, y'know...."

He hesitated a moment, and then went on almost apologetically:

"Jis' wanted to tell ya. 'Tain't no skin off my backside anyhow. Daytimes I work at the plant; nights I drink my beer. Don't cut no ice with me one way or t'other. Jis' wanted to tell ya, that's all...."

I was on my feet too and was suddenly aware that I had clasped the hand of Old Man Manseau. I cannot say whether he realized how I felt. Not likely. Anyway, he gave no sign of it. Of course his warning had taught me nothing I did not know. I was quite aware of what to expect. But I was touched by his good-will, by the feeling of comradeship, perhaps even of support, that Old Man Manseau had sought to convey – the fellow-feeling of a mere beer-parlour acquaintance, looked down upon as an alcoholic by the righteous citizenry. He spared me further embarrassment by lifting his two fingers to the peak of his leather cap.

"See ya agin, Monsieur Jodoin – and take it easy, eh?"

And he lurched away, bobbling stiffly like a jumping-jack on his widespread unsteady legs.

My agitation left me as quickly as it had come – fortunately, for I dislike emotion. Besides, having drunk my fill I was immune to the slings and arrows of the outside world. I was in that soothing condition where the whole situation struck me as rather comical. Yet my mind was clear. I understood better than ever the exasperation of M. Chicoine. If my run-in with the priest and the student had become common knowledge, might not the book shop be facing the loss of its whole ecclesiastical trade – a good forty per cent of the total? A fair number of laymen would obviously follow the lead of the clergy.... This thought brought a smile to my lips. Léon Chicoine would be in a fine mess. In fact he was already in it. That would teach him to load me with extra work, with his confounded *sanctum sanctorum*, and then treat me like an office boy.... Of course I realized too that I might anticipate a few unpleasant moments myself. But you never get anything for nothing.

The clock said a quarter to one, but thanks to Old Man Manseau I was already on my feet, so I decided to go on home. The walk would limber up my brain as well as my legs.

May 8

For the first time since my arrival in Saint Joachim I am getting some scribbling done on a week-day. The fact is that since Sunday matters have been coming to a head, so to speak.

In the first place I have patched things up with Rose. Hence I was in a position to know that she would be out this evening: some bingo party or other at the parish hall. Perhaps she hoped I would go with her. But there is a limit to my spirit of accommodation. Besides, it is always unwise to appear too eager after a reconciliation. I say "reconciliation" for lack of a better term. When you come right down to it we had not really quarrelled; a bit of coolness, nothing more.

That is why she waited several days before seeking me out. Even then it had taken "an urgent reason". But let us get down to the facts. Two days after Old Man Manseau's warning, I came back to my room at the usual time, that is to say about ten after one in the morning, to find, to my surprise, Rose sitting in my armchair waiting for me. I admit I was a little high at the time, but not so far gone as to imagine that she was there because of my irresistible charms. Besides, she very soon made everything clear to me by announcing in tragic tones:

"I've heard about what's going on, Monsieur Jodoin. And when I found out that people were trying to do you dirt, I decided to wait up for you."

I wondered how much had reached her ears, whether perhaps she knew even more about it than I did, and whether some thunderbolt was about to strike me. However, as I was sleepy, and anxious to take my Safe-All salts because of a certain tingling in the bladder, I was in no mood to press her for details. So I confined myself to the statement that I was touched by her concern, but that, as far as I knew, nobody was trying to "do me dirt". Unfortunately this reply served only to redouble her solicitude. After first assuring me that her sole aim was to help me, she expressed the fear that I did not fully realize the seriousness of the situation. Not having lived in Saint Joachim as long as she had, I could not hope to appreciate the wickedness of certain people and the vicious destructiveness of their gossip.

"I know what it's like, believe me!" she went on, disappointed at my imperturbability. "When I had to leave my husband – because he was really impossible, the filthy beast – don't imagine that it was any bed of roses. You should just have heard them blabber!... Believe it or not, it reached the point where I was almost afraid to show myself in the street.... The way people looked at me!....I didn't know which way to turn...."

I shrugged indifferently, thinking to myself that it would

take more than nasty looks to upset the routine of my life.

"But don't you know what's going on?" she asked excitedly. "Hasn't anybody told you anything?"

I replied that every day several people uttered a certain number of words in my presence, but that if she would be so kind as to state precisely what she was referring to, I might be in a better position to give her a relevant reply to her question. She did not wait to be asked twice.

"You mean you don't know there is a clique here in Saint Joachim that has sworn to get you fired and to run you out of town? It's exactly the same bunch that tried to get rid of me when circumstances drove me to leave my husband...."

I confessed that I was not aware of this supposed conspiracy, but added that if one were to heed all the rumours that circulated in a small town there would be time for nothing else.

Mme Bouthiller paused a moment trying to think up a decisive argument. Then she spread out her arms in a helpless gesture and said in a weary voice:

"You really don't realize how serious the situation is. If you had gone through what I have, you wouldn't take things so lightly...."

This discussion was beginning to annoy me, the more so as I was now starting to wake up, which meant I was in for a night of insomnia. But how could I say that to her? I resolved to bear my cross patiently, and declared to Rose that naturally I did not know what she had "gone through" but that, as she was younger than I, it was reasonable to suppose that I had "gone through" as many trials as she had.

This comment failed to take her fancy. She declared vehemently that I had better start thinking right away about how to defend myself against the evil tongues that were bent on ruining me. Léon Chicoine would ask nothing better than to make me the goat. He was a hypocrite, a Pharisee who hid his immoral intrigues behind a façade of respectability. But I must not allow myself to be walked on. I must go to the presbytery and explain to the priest the true situation "from beginning to end".

Rose did not seem to know exactly what the "true situation" was, but her attitude indicated that she was eager to find out. So when I answered that it was not my custom to frequent presbyteries, especially for the futile purpose of clearing myself of imaginary faults, she looked extremely disappointed. She did not for a moment suppose I was guilty, she said. The important thing was to defend myself against these accusations. Did I want to be known as a corrupter of schoolboys?

"I know perfectly well that it's only gossip," she went on, in a tone still not entirely free from a shade of doubt, "but not everybody is like me, for goodness' sake! There are people who believe that because a man bends his elbow once in a while he is capable of anything; that it's only a step from taking a drink to corruption of the young. Don't you understand?"

What I understood was that I was beginning to get hot under the collar. What really got me was that Mme Bouthiller herself seemed just a bit inclined to place some credence in this gossip. Just to set things straight, I pointed out that if I had wanted to "corrupt schoolboys", as she had so happily put it, I should probably not have set up my headquarters at Trefflé's. A few of the younger set did drop in there on occasion, but the regular customers were all men of middle age or well past. Furthermore, aside from the two waiters, I had never once spoken to anyone at Trefflé's except Old Man Manseau – who, in sober truth, could not be described either as young or as a schoolboy.

Feeling that her good faith was being impugned, Rose became indignant. Really I was determined not to understand! It was not at *Chez Trefflé* that I was being accused of carrying on my campaign of immorality, but at Léon Chicoine's book shop. As she uttered the name of my boss Rose became still more agitated. It was obvious she nursed an old grudge against him. He was, she warned me, a snake-in-the-grass who pulled off his dirty little tricks in secret, who made clever advances to women (but never in front of witnesses), who belonged to several civic and religious organizations, thereby acquiring such influence that the parish priest, despite his dislike for him, hesitated to attack him head-on. But when it came to a poor woman like herself, forced into a separation by a husband "as low as anybody can get", then the evil tongues wagged at full speed, and nobody felt any obligation to spare her feelings. That was why, battle-weary, Mme Bouthiller had eventually had to go and see the priest. This had not really patched everything up, but the situation was now more tolerable. Since then she had been rigorous in discharging her religious duties, and that in itself was a guarantee of relative peace and quiet. And so on.

I must admit that her tirade, though a bit confused, was not lacking in interest. It cast new light on the personality of Léon Chicoine. As for trying to weigh the merits of these assertions, I gave it no thought. Ascribing my silence to hesitation, Rose renewed the attack. I simply had to go and see the priest. According to her this was the only solution. She had tried it herself. She knew.

At this, my irritation once more broke surface. Her case and mine, I asserted, were entirely different. In the first place, I had it on good authority that the priest considered me feeble-minded. In the second place, I found religious services boring and I had no use for them. And in the third place, the Joachimites, with all their old wives' tales, could not deny me entry to Trefflé's, so I didn't care a rap. And so on.

The discussion stretched out for a good hour, both of us

re-hashing the same arguments, neither convincing the other. The whole business ended, fittingly enough, in bed. Rose wanted to be near me "in my hour of need". I offered no protest, but in the morning I was literally demolished.

About nine o'clock the same day I had just settled myself on my stool with the hope of catching a few winks, when a young fellow appeared bearing a sealed envelope from Milord Chicoine. As I looked surprised, he explained in a very loud voice that M. Chicoine was in Saint Jules on business. Being unable to get in touch with me before leaving, he was sending me his instructions in writing. A glance about the room assured me that my fellow-employees had followed this speech with great interest. The old girls sensed that something was in the wind, as the saying has it. I opened the envelope and read the following:

Join me as quickly as you can at 114 Saint Lin Road (in the suburbs). Say nothing to the others. Take a taxi. It's urgent.
Léon Chicoine.
P.S. I'll reimburse you for the trip.

I slipped the note into my pocket and assured the messenger that I would follow orders to the letter. A few minutes later I calmly announced to the old maids that, following instructions from M. Chicoine, I should have to go out for a while. Mlle Galarneau demanded tartly who was to look after the book department during my absence. I answered that I had no idea, inasmuch as M. Chicoine had left me no directives on the matter. She retorted that she would have no part of it. She knew too well, she went on, the sort of thing people exposed themselves to in selling books. A person would have to be an inexperienced newcomer to take on so dangerous an assign-

74

ment. I was tempted to remind her that, if my memory did not betray me, her own brother, the rural mail-man, had nevertheless sought this perilous position before my arrival. But what was the good of provoking any more hatred than necessary? I merely shrugged, then put on my coat and went out.

Once outside, I perceived that the weather was fine. I was surprised: ordinarily I pay no attention to the temperature unless it is extreme and uncomfortable. Even then it is purely a sensory impression which does not penetrate my consciousness. But no matter. That particular morning the sun had caught the street on the flank and inflamed the shop windows. Perhaps it was this dazzling reflection that brought me out of my shell and allowed me to take in the intense blue of the sky, which was soft as silk and dotted with tiny round clouds like puffs of pipe smoke. The sensation was so new, so powerful, that I paused a moment in admiration. Those who are frequently touched by such a feeling are fortunate. At least, I suppose they are. But then ugliness must distress them, too, so perhaps the whole thing balances up. But no matter.

I brought my eyes back to the shop fronts which stretched to the vanishing point on both sides of the street. There it was less beautiful. Lacking reflections, they remained nothing more than rows of rather shabby store fronts, revamped in the modern manner and set awkwardly into buildings of blackened brick. But why all these details? Could it be that I am loath to get on with my story? It is true that what follows is not particularly savoury. No matter. Let us proceed.

I made my way to a taxi-stand in the main street and gave the driver the address. It was quite far off, and I understood why M. Chicoine had suggested a cab. Within a few minutes we were running through open country, and I found it difficult to believe that we had not left the municipality. There was a good acre of ground between the houses. The driver could not often have gone so far afield. On three different occasions he asked me whether I was sure of the address, and when we stopped in front of the farm – for such it was – he asked me again. I replied confidently that this was the place all right. He offered to wait anyway until the door opened, but I told him not to bother, and I remained standing beside the car until he made up his mind to move off.

Then I went round the house and knocked at the back door. In the country this is customary, as I knew. It was M. Chicoine himself who let me in. I believe I have already noted that he has a naturally waxy complexion. But on that particular morning it was positively grotesque: the words greenish or cadaverous would describe it better. Fatigue had cut deep wrinkles into his brow and channelled every plane of his face. His chin displayed a fungus of yellowish stubble, and the whites of his eyes were streaked with fibrous red veins. It was clear that he had not slept a wink all night, and this thought cheered me considerably. He shook my hand with a feverish gesture as though I were an old friend he had not seen for years. As I have said, this was a farm-house, and a single large room occupied the whole ground floor. There was an old couple occupying a pair of rocking-chairs near the far window, but, without stopping to introduce me to them, M. Chicoine pushed me upstairs into a bedroom heated by a small oil-burner. Only when he had installed himself opposite me in a leather-bottomed chair did he open his mouth to announce in a voice filled with tragedy:

"Martin Guérard has betrayed us!"

I clucked sympathetically, all the while racking my brain to remember who Martin Guérard might be. Was he the student to whom I had sold the *Essay on Morals*? This seemed possible, but I was puzzled by this talk of a "betrayal". The most expeditious procedure, of course, would have been to ask for details. But M. Chicoine had delivered his announcement in such pathetic tones, with the obvious aim of casting me into his own deep depression, that I dared not disillusion him.

"What do you suggest?" he inquired, after a pause.

I shrugged, raised my eyebrows, and tossed off the remark that the said Martin Guérard was perhaps not considered so reliable a witness as to make his declarations unassailable.

"That's what I told myself at the start!" exclaimed M. Chicoine. "But the precise details he has furnished remove all hope from that angle."

Being mindful of the bitterness with which the boss had referred to Guérard, I declared resoundingly that the fellow was a scoundrel. M. Chicoine interrupted me with a gesture.

"Come now, Monsieur Jodoin, we mustn't be too hard!"

I reiterated in a still more affirmative tone that Guérard was a scoundrel. Such a statement committed me to nothing, and I was still hopeful that M. Chicoine's replies would shed some light on the object of my invective.

"I'm not of your opinion, Monsieur Jodoin," he went on in a pontifical tone. "In the first place, a customer who makes a purchase in a book shop has no obligation to conceal the origin of his acquisition. There is no question here of clandestine or illegal trade. No doubt you will argue that in the present case Guérard knew very well that noising the transaction abroad would be bound to get us into hot water. I agree. But on the other hand don't forget that, until the fathers threatened him with expulsion, young Guérard, it seems, staunchly insisted that he had found the volume in the school yard...."

I uttered a sigh of relief. So the culprit was indeed my schoolboy. Catching M. Chicoine's quizzical stare, I conceded that, without entirely exculpating Martin Guérard, these were certainly mitigating circumstances.

"Precisely!" exclaimed M. Chicoine, who must have turned the problem over in his mind a hundred times. "Precisely! You can hardly apply the term 'scoundrel' to a mere boy who managed to withstand several days' pressure from the school authorities.... Of course, if they had swallowed his rather naïve little tale of having found the book in the yard, that would have suited him just as well as ourselves. But unfortunately for us this Guérard is known as 'a dangerous reader, as well as a budding anti-clerical' – these are the very words of the Father Superior.... So of course, with a reputation like that, the good fathers naturally gave him the third degree... with the result you know."

These words seemed to bring home to him the bitterness of the situation, for he sighed again endlessly:

"Father Bonet himself telephoned the news to me last night...."

M. Chicoine fixed me with his bloodshot eyes. Seeing that I awaited the sequel without flinching, he went on:

"It means they have the knife at my throat. It was urgent to find a hiding-place where I could *consult* you" (he emphasized that word), "so as to work out a solution...."

He paused to clear the frog in his throat several times before resuming:

"On the telephone, of course, I pretended to be surprised and incredulous. I told Father Bonet that I had to go to Saint Jules tomorrow – that is today – on business, but that I would look into the matter as soon as I got back. This morning at five o'clock I jumped into my car – it's hidden in the implement shed – and I came out here.... There!" he concluded, with a gesture that brought his skinny arms up to the level of his shoulders. "Now you know everything. I've put my cards on the table."

I was not too clear on the sense to be attached to the

expression "cards on the table", which suggests the idea of opposition, not to say rivalry. So I adopted the strategy of praising M. Chicoine for his presence of mind in the face of the priest's phone call, as well as for the astuteness he had displayed in arranging this interview in an isolated farmhouse. M. Chicoine responded to this flattery by relaxing his frown slightly and resuming in an insinuating tone:

"You realize, I'm sure, my friend – for you are my friend, aren't you? I can hardly consider you a mere employee after the trials we have undergone together. You are, aren't you?" he insisted.

I was amazed that a reasonably intelligent adult could bring himself to ask so idiotic a question. However, I dutifully assured him that our friendship was of course undying.

"Fine, my friend, fine!" he exclaimed. "Well then, let me repeat my question, just between friends: you realize, don't you, what a catastrophic situation I find myself in? . . . I'm not accusing or blaming anyone, you understand. I'm just asking you a simple question."

I pointed out to him that my slight experience in the business world and my limited grasp of the Joachimite mentality did not enable me to reach a judgment on the nature, catastrophic or otherwise, of current developments. I added, however, that I supposed the clerical trade of the book shop would perhaps undergo a mild recession.

At these words M. Chicoine smote his brow with a resounding smack which I immediately suspected was not intended as a tribute to my intelligence.

"A mild recession!" he howled, waving his arms wildly. "A 'mild recession', you say?"

He was beside himself and his eyes were like daggers. Did I really imagine, he bellowed, that this would be the extent of the damage? Such blindness was beyond description, and could come only from stupidity or from bad faith. How was it possible, after so much as a single day in Saint Joachim, for anybody to entertain such wild delusions about the outlook of the citizenry?

I realized that M. Chicoine was no longer in full possession of his faculties, as the saying goes. Unfortunately his frenzy of stuttering prevented my seizing all the shades of meaning incorporated in his tirade, which in itself was not lacking in interest. I did understand, nevertheless, that over the past twenty years a veiled animosity had been developing between the parish priest of Saint Joachim and the fathers of Saint Roch School. About 1930, in fact, the aforementioned school had erected a new chapel capable of holding at least four times the number of its students. Sensing danger, Father Bonet had appeared at the site of operations several times to express to the good fathers his astonishment at the "colossal" dimensions of the future edifice. The school authorities had spoken vaguely of the foresight necessary in administering an institution situated close to a parish like Saint Joachim, a parish in full development and guided by a firm and competent hand. The parish priest had returned to his presbytery reassured. But six months later, once the chapel was finished and duly consecrated by the bishop, several Joachimites had fallen into the habit of going to the new chapel to discharge their religious duties. The Sunday collections of Saint Joachim had suffered in consequence a humiliating and painful decrease. Father Bonet had unleashed several sermons directed against "certain so-called religious movements" whose true aim was, it appeared, to undermine venerable parochial organizations almost three centuries old. His objurgations had remained without effect, the more so as the staff of the school chanced just then to acquire a first-rate preacher, whose sermons – humorous, but unimpeachably orthodox – elicited lusty guffaws from the good Joachimites, who crowded into the new chapel. Upon the death of Father Rivard, as he was called, chance had once more favoured the school administration, who again produced an eloquent and witty preacher to replace him and carry on the tradition. Father Bonet fulminated in vain from the height of his own pulpit; his voice was drowned in the outbursts of laughter emanating from the school chapel.

M. Chicoine interrupted his account to dab his brow with a grimy handkerchief. The events he had been reporting, however amusing in themselves, seemed to bring him no great joy. For my own part, I had lit up one of my acrid little Italian cigars (I don't like them much, but they have the significant advantage of inducing fits of coughing in those who talk to me), and I was waiting for what might follow. After another sigh, M. Chicoine went on in a cavernous voice:

"If all I had to worry about were either the priest or the fathers alone, I'd have some chance of getting out of it. A few protestations of ignorance, a few promises to exercise more vigilance over the sale of my books, and in the long run things could be patched up...."

But on the contrary he found himself literally between two fires. The artillery on both sides was in position and he, Léon Chicoine, occupied no-man's-land. The school fathers could hardly fail to exploit their advantage to the full. The book shop was situated in the town of Saint Joachim, within a stone's throw of the presbytery itself; and consequently within the moral purview of the parish priest. And forbidden books were being sold there under his very eyes! It was predictable that on the following Sunday the Saint Roch chapel would resound with witty and corrosive insinuations. Good Father Dugas was no doubt busily sharpening his arrows.... Being properly cornered, what could Father Bonet do but strike hard? And against whom? Against Léon Chicoine, proprietor of the book shop that bore his name....

At these words the boss struck his fist against his skinny chest, which returned a hollow echo. He seemed on the verge of tears:

"I am a ruined man, Monsieur Jodoin!" he proclaimed melodramatically. "You realize what that means? A ruined man, with a wife and six children to support!"

His piteous air begged some kind of response.

I confessed that, not being married, and having no children so far as I was aware, it was no doubt difficult for me to put myself entirely in his place. When it came to the subject of ruined men, however, I felt myself not entirely without understanding. In fact I placed myself in that category, in the sense that I no longer hoped to attain any degree of success in life, whether intellectual, social, financial, or merely matrimonial....

M. Chicoine did not allow me to continue. Pressing my hand paternally between both of his own (which were cold and sticky) he burst out.

"Then you can sympathize with my position! I didn't for a moment doubt your goodness of heart!"

I pointed out that it was not a question of goodness of heart but of the understanding of life that came from a certain number of rather disagreeable experiences. But it was no use: M. Chicoine was in no mood to listen. He declared in a quavering voice that the wisdom of my words proved to him that my life, far from being finished, held the promise of happy times and unhoped-for successes. I thanked him for his kind words and affirmed that no one would be more delighted than myself if his predictions turned out to be correct.

Though reiterating his "absolute confidence in my future",

M. Chicoine saw fit to emphasize that perhaps Saint Joachim was not the ideal field of activity for a man like me: enlightened, brilliant, vastly cultured, devoted to individual freedom, etc., etc. He laid it on thick, and of course it was clear to me that he was loosing upon me some of the oiliest blarney it had ever been my lot to hear. My admiration for this exhibition did not blind me to the fact that I had just been given my walking-papers. At the same time, the circumlocutions in which the boss had couched his announcement brought home to me that I held a few trumps myself, as the saying goes. Nobody shoots off his face at that rate just for the fun of it.

I resolved, therefore, to sell my skin dearly. I protested that his friendship for me had blinded him to my obvious faults. It was twenty years at least, I went on, since I had given up all notion that I was called to a high destiny, to use a common phrase, and my peregrinations upon the surface of the globe appeared to me to be utterly devoid of meaning. I added that in Saint Joachim I had acquired a certain little routine to which, in a sense, I was rathèr attached, inasmuch as it always demands more effort to change one's habits than to keep on with them.

"You haven't entirely grasped my meaning," M. Chicoine resumed in a soft voice. "Even if you stay in Saint Joachim – and naturally you are at liberty to do so – your habits will be upset to some extent. Don't you agree? That's inevitable when you change jobs. For of course I shall be compelled, if not to close my doors entirely – though that too is possible –, to reduce my staff considerably, and perhaps to eliminate my book department altogether... assuming that I can avoid an early bankruptcy...."

He rubbed his stubbly chin and observed me critically before going on.

"There might perhaps be one way to avert disaster. I mention it on the off-chance.... It's as good as any other method. If it succeeded, we'd be pulling the wool over the eyes of certain . . . personages whose ideas, if I'm not mistaken, you find objectionable. Right?"

I replied that, if he would take the trouble to explain precisely what he was getting at, I should be delighted to answer his question. At this, M. Chicoine's features relaxed:

"Fine! I was sure we'd come to an understanding. . . . The people I mean are the ones who are trying to . . . to place obstacles in the path of individual freedom, of freedom of thought. . . . You get the point?"

I nodded.

"And you are opposed to those obstacles?"

I assured him that I was in favour of freedom.

"Well then, does it strike you as exactly . . . normal that you and I are forced by circumstances to meet and talk here in secret because of an action which is in no way contrary to the law of the land?"

I agreed that such circumstances were not normal; that on the contrary they were intolerable, and that it was only because we had both lived since childhood in this atmosphere of constraint that we failed to react to the aforementioned circumstances with the indignation they deserved. Anyway, I added, I saw no real reason for burying ourselves in the depths of the country like this rather than discussing the question right out in the open – at Trefflé's, for example, or at the book shop.

M. Chicoine replied excitedly that this was no more than a tactical retreat. Soon we should carry out a sortie that would take the enemy in completely. Was I agreed?

I refused to commit myself before knowing the nature of the manoeuvre he had in mind, but I felt disposed to greet the proposal with sympathy.

M. Chicoine bent toward me, and I could tell from his breath that he had been drinking. In an excited voice that stumbled over the syllables he began to set forth his plan. At first I thought I must be misunderstanding him. His previous boastfulness, his belligerent expressions, had suggested to my mind a daring and spectacular expedition. Instead what was he proposing? – a vulgar, sheepish little scheme with an air of sneak-thievery about it. I realized then that, with all his bombast, Léon Chicoine was nothing but a snivelling weakling disembowelled with fear, clinging for dear life to his little business.

Overcoming my disgust I pleaded with him lengthily, invoking every argument I could think of that might induce him to modify his project. Nothing had any effect. I found myself on the horns of a dilemma: either I carried out the plan, at some small profit to me, or else I refused on grounds of principle, leaving the task to another and getting nothing out of it for myself. Only the threat of denouncing him to the parish priest or to the school fathers could have swayed Chicoine – and such an act would have debased me even below his own level.

So after an hour of stormy debate, I agreed to fall in with his plan, in consideration of a payment of five hundred dollars, plus expenses of course. He put on the countenance of an impaled martyr, but handed me half the agreed sum and promised to have the balance delivered to me "on the spot".

As I rose to leave, he offered me his hand. I ignored it and went out without a word.

May 10

It is all over. Anyway, I presume it is, and I find
myself wondering why I bother to set down these last details in
my diary. Long-standing professional disease, no doubt. It is
true that I am still feeling a little out of my element, and writing
helps to pass some of the time. But no matter.

After leaving Chicoine the day before yesterday (the day
before yesterday? – it seems an eternity since I lit out of Saint
Joachim), I went right back to my room and packed my
suitcase, a dog-eared Gladstone bag of blackish leather dap-
pled with ancient water-marks. I had no wish to see Rose again
before leaving. I did not know whether my farewells would
have provoked a scene, but in any case it was better to avoid the
risk. So I packed up, which took only a few minutes. For some
time to come I should not have to fuss about my appearance, as

the saying goes, so I shoved my clothes pell-mell into the suitcase and stood on it long enough to get an old belt round it.

Having nothing more to do until after dark, I went round to Trefflé's where my appearance at this unaccustomed hour, above all with a travelling bag in my hand, caused a new sensation. To forestall any circuitous inquiries, I immediately told Fred, the waiter, that I was leaving that very evening on a business trip on behalf of M. Chicoine. To lend credence to this tale, I asked Fred whether he was familiar with the bus schedules. I explained that I had to be in Montreal the next morning in time for the opening of the book shops. The waiter went to the trouble of telephoning the bus terminal. The last bus left at one-thirty in the morning and arrived in Montreal at five a.m. I remarked that this was a bit early, but would do. I took down this item of information in a notebook, which seemed to reassure Fred as to the truth of my assertions. As a matter of fact, one-thirty in the morning suited me perfectly. My appointment was set for two o'clock. I could leave the beer parlour at my usual hour, more or less, take a little walk to clear my head, and still get where I was going at the time agreed upon.

The only thing was that my session at Trefflé's was beginning seven hours earlier than usual so I had to slow down the pace of my ingurgitations. I acquitted myself honourably, if I do say so myself. At one in the morning, I was neither more nor less tipsy than was customary with me. The only variation from my usual habits was to gulp down a cup of coffee before leaving. Old Man Manseau was still at his post when I rose to go. Without quite knowing why, I stopped in front of him and stretched out my hand. He got to his feet and for a moment or two my own hand was grasped in the calloused palm of the machinist. I am sure he understood that I was leaving for good, for he spoke up in his gruff voice:

"So long, there, Monsieur Jodoin. And good luck t'ye, heh? Good luck."

I was really moved. He was the only Joachimite for whom I felt any kinship. Calm, stoical, taciturn, he struck me as much wiser than people who get all worked up. At that moment I regretted not having developed a closer acquaintance with this table neighbour of three months' standing. Now it was too late. I said good-bye in my turn, and went out.

Was it only after I was outside, with the wind whipping my face and clearing my mind, that my own scheme began to take root in my brain? Or had it been brewing unconsciously during my session in the beer parlour? Hard to say. Anyway, it makes no difference. It is difficult enough to remember one's actions without trying to dredge up their psychological origins. All I know for sure is that by the time I reached the back door of the book shop my mind was made up. The truck driver, an iron-jawed gorilla dressed in leather cap and jacket, was already waiting for me beside his Ford. He looked a bit worried.

"Are you the fella about the books?" he asked, as soon as he caught sight of me.

I replied that I was indeed the fellow about the books, at which he grunted approvingly and started toward the shop. I told him that we could not begin until precisely two o'clock, because I was waiting for a note from M. Chicoine. I could have set him to work right away. With or without the expected envelope (which was to contain the two hundred and fifty dollars still coming to me) my mind was made up.

As it turned out, the messenger was right on time. I waited until he had disappeared again before opening the shop. The driver had brought along an electric lantern, which I placed on the floor, and a quantity of cardboard cartons. I unlocked the *sanctum sanctorum*. While the gorilla began to pack the books I checked the contents of the envelope. It was all there. I sank into Chicoine's tilting chair behind the desk and dozed off for a good spell with my elbows on the writing-pad. It was the driver who woke me up:

"That the lot?"

I stretched my stiffened limbs and went to inspect the *sanctum sanctorum*. The shelves were empty. I told the trucker that that would do, slipped the padlock into my pocket, locked the back door of the shop and got into the truck. It was a two-ton Ford, in fairly good condition, covered with a brown tarpaulin. We moved off smoothly. The gorilla was a good driver. I let him roll along for a few minutes before inquiring in a neutral tone whether he knew where we were bound for.

"Sure enough," he replied, "we're goin' to Sainte Cécile."

"Sainte Cécile!" I exclaimed. "Did M. Chicoine tell you Sainte Cécile? When did you talk to him last?"

The driver had not spoken to M. Chicoine himself. It was the owner of the truck, a certain Jules Matteau, who had arranged the details of our enterprise with the boss. We were on our way to his farm.

"So that's it!" I exclaimed, with an understanding nod. "Now I see what's happened. M. Chicoine didn't have time to let M. Matteau know, or else M. Matteau wasn't able to get in touch with you. . . . We're going to Montreal."

"To Montreal?"

The murmur of the engine dropped a tone. The gorilla scratched his head beneath his wilted leather cap and threw me a suspicious glance. He turned the problem over in his mind and finally declared:

"Montreal! That ain't quite so near-by as Sainte Cécile, y'know."

I corroborated this judgment; but he felt impelled to pursue his syllogism to its ultimate conclusion:

"When it's further off, it takes more gas an' more time."

Once more I went along with his statement of the case, adding that what we had to do now was figure out how much extra gas and time would be required to go to Montreal instead of to Sainte Cécile.

The chubby fingers of the driver once more raked away at his narrow skull. He had only the vaguest notions about the route to Montreal. He had been there once with a pal a few years before, but had not paid much attention to the itinerary. According to him, the distance could be as much as two hundred miles. But it might well be a hundred miles more than that. In short, he did not want to commit himself. The one thing he was sure of was that it was certainly going to cost more.

After rather lengthy bargaining, it was agreed that, if we reached our destination before eight o'clock, the price would be seventy-five dollars; if not, it would cost ten dollars for each extra hour. Once convinced that I was ready to pay cash on arrival, the gorilla did not open his mouth again, save to ask for directions from time to time.

At the Sénésac Book Store in Montreal everything went off well. I knew the proprietor, having met him once or twice at the *Cercle des amis du livre* in the days when I still used to hob-nob with that sort of crowd. At first sight he failed to recognize me. I must have looked pretty seedy. Quite customary with me, I agree, but that morning it must have been worse than usual. It should not be forgotten that I had spent a sleepless night, first tippling in a beer parlour and subsequently riding in the cab of a truck which had sought out with pitiless springs every bump in the road. Of course I had not shaved, and my beard is thick-set and very black in spite of my greying hair. In short, I had to say who I was and name some mutual acquaintances before Sénésac would consent to talk business.

To whet his interest I emphasized the urgent nature of this trip, inasmuch as certain Jansenistic Joachimites were at that moment preparing to launch a kind of raid on Léon's Book Shop, and to boycott it mercilessly ever after if they came across so much as a single suspicious volume. At the same time I pointed out that the urgency applied only to the evacuation of the books, not to their immediate disposal. If necessary they could always be put in storage. Sénésac then agreed – "just to do me a favour" – to "have a look" at my cargo. Having rummaged through the cartons, he assumed a rather disdainful look and asked the price. I urged upon him that the books were worth two thousand dollars at the very least, but added that in view of the circumstances my boss, being reasonable and a realist, would let them go for fifteen hundred. We concluded the deal at seven hundred and eighty. All things considered, this was not a bad price. I paid off the gorilla, who stuffed the money in his pocket and made off without a word.

I felt myself unburdened of a great weight. My little deal had killed two birds with one stone: I had outwitted the bigwigs of Saint Joachim and at the same time taken in that gutless Pharisee Chicoine – not to mention the twelve hundred-odd dollars I had in my pocket, a small fortune that would allow me to live without worry for perhaps a whole year.

Naturally I propose to go over to the Employment Office again and draw the unemployment insurance to which I am now entitled. The one hitch is that they might find me a job. But you can always arrange to get turned down by behaving like a boor or an idiot. Preferably an idiot. This keeps the bureaucrats from smelling a rat, for prospective employers tend in such cases to report rather vaguely on their reasons for rejecting an applicant. They do not push their altruism to the point of hiring one of the "retarded" themselves (there are such smooth terms these days to designate imbecility), but they balk at ruining his chances of finding something elsewhere.

In short, no worries on that score. Nor on the score of Chicoine either, for that matter. He must be fuming with rage, of course. I certainly hope so: a character who invokes great principles of liberty, for which he gives not a tinker's damn, solely for the purpose of filling his sock! Yes, he must be howling his head off. But his hands are tied. If he attempted to lay charges against me, I should be in a position to unleash "catastrophic" reprisals, to use his expression. Anyway, I am not worried. He will not lift a finger. He will write off the *sanctum sanctorum* to profit and loss, while charging me, for the benefit of anyone who will listen, with sole responsibility for the sale of the *Essay on Morals*. No matter.

As for me, I shall have to try to break myself in to some new habits. Without a well-marked little routine to follow, one does too much thinking, which is unpleasant. I am sure everything will be going smoothly inside a week or two. I have found myself a suitable room, which is a beginning. When I say "suitable" I mean that it costs me only eighteen dollars a month; all else is of little importance. In addition I have bought myself an old armchair from a Craig Street second-hand dealer. It is to be delivered shortly. It may also be necessary to get another mattress, for the one I now have presents a rather uneven terrain. But then it may be that I shall get used to it. Anyway, I shall soon know where I stand; a week or two more, perhaps...

In a way I am sorry to bring this diary to a close. Of course I could start another one. But what for? Montreal is not Saint Joachim. Here, there are other ways of killing time, even on Sundays.